ANTELOPE SPRINGS

ANTELOPE SPRINGS

G. Clifton Wisler

Walker and Company
New York

A-1

for my sister Karen,
with love

First published in the United States of America
in 1986 by the Walker Publishing Company, Inc.

Published simultaneously in Canada by John Wiley & Sons
Canada, Limited, Rexdale, Ontario.

Library of Congress Cataloging-in-Publication Data

Wisler, G. Clifton.
  Antelope Springs.

  I. Title.
PS3573.I877A5   1986   813'.54   86-15680
ISBN 0-8027-4062-6

Printed in the United States of America

10   9   8   7   6   5   4   3   2   1

CHAPTER 1

ANTELOPE Springs painted a narrow strip of green across the gray landscape of western Texas. There, some thirty miles from the Brazos crossings, flowed three perpetually bubbling springs. A deep pool of water collected at the base of Calvary Hill. Once it had been a favorite camping ground for the free-roaming Indians of the southwestern plain. In 1874, following Mackenzie's triumph over Quannah Parker and the last of the die-hard Comanches, a way station had been established at the Springs.

The station served as a remount post for the Overland Stage. Occasionally, when a wheel went bad or the weather turned from miserable to impossible, stagecoach passengers were housed for the night in the rear of the station-house. Other times the stage would stop only long enough for passengers to buy a hot meal. Salted beef and biscuits could be purchased for the long journey ahead.

By 1880, the station had passed through the hands of three owners. Old Lucien DeVries, who'd first settled the land after wresting it away from the Indians, had gone on to his reward. His daughter Katherine and her husband, Bill Merritt, found their ranch and the neighboring station too much to handle so they sold the Springs and a thousand acres to Everett Raymond.

Ev Raymond had spent four years in the Confederate cavalry, three more working horses at his brother's ranch and a decade as marshal of Jacksboro. All that left him longing for the peace and solitude of the far frontier. On a summer's day two long years ago, he'd loaded his wife and four children into a wagon and set out for the station he'd just bought from the Merritts.

"God, help us," Susan Raymond had cried when she first saw the place. The waterhole had been fouled by straying cattle and horses. Two pigs ran amuck through the house, and the barn had collapsed during a spring thunderstorm. But by autumn a fine stable had been built of oak planks, a new barn was finished and ready for fall hay, and the old two-room cabin had been extended to include a storeroom, large dining room, three bedrooms for the family and two more for guests. A separate kitchen and outhouse were constructed out back, and a loft provided bedding space for the children in the event of extra guests.

The following spring Ev and the boys had dug a diversion ditch from the springs to the horse corral, then fenced in the waterhole to ward off unwelcome visitors. Susan cleared land and planted a vegetable garden, and Ev purchased a hundred head of cattle from the Merritts.

"As for horses, they're all over these hills," Bill Merritt explained. "Been runnin' free since the Spanish first set foot in this country."

So Ev and young Martin had embarked on their first mustang hunt, spending half of June in the hills and returning with two dozen wild ponies. Once broken to saddle, the horses became the Raymonds' prime cash crop. Income from the station paid the note Ev had signed to the bank in Weatherford for the balance of the purchase price for the land.

This was their third summer at Antelope Springs and the note was two-thirds paid. Another good sale at the horse auction in Weatherford, put together with the station income, would pay the balance.

"That's the thing about havin' land with water on it," Bill Merritt said often. "The drought never catches a man short who's got water."

Still Ev dreaded the lean years which came to the neighboring farms and ranches. There'd be little money for travel, and even less for buying horses. The cattle markets would be flooded with beeves, and the price would fall through the floor. But spring rains had been heavy, and all signs pointed to a banner year.

A man didn't deserve to be so much at peace with himself and his world, Ev thought. There it was, summer, and they were all sound of limb and unusually even-tempered. Even little Todd had set aside his pestering of Rachel, although it was deep in the nature of ten-year-olds to test the patience of their younger sisters. Finley had settled into one of those serious moods that plague boys of twelve.

And Martin had been like an extra right arm to Ev from the moment they'd left Jacksboro. He was like his mother, steady as a beaver, yet full of laughter and always ready with a surprise. It seemed strange to Ev that Martin, who resembled Susan less than the rest of the children, should have so much of her soul in him—perhaps it was because Ev had been gone so often those first few years of Martin's life.

"Stage's due in," Martin said, looking out across the expansive plain.

Ev smiled. Lately Martin kept up with the stage schedule better than anyone. Of course, the stages weren't all that good at keeping to their schedules, but it helped Susan to know what days to expect guests for dinner.

"Son, why don't you take the fresh team out for a little air. Then put 'em in the ready corral."

"Yes, sir."

Martin led the first of the four big grays that made up the relief team for the westbound stage.

"How's the right forefoot on Star?" Ev asked, watching

the animal with a five-pointed splash of white across her forehead.

"Seems fair enough to me," Martin answered. "She'll do fine."

Ev sighed. There was a second relief team in the stable, four black dancers kept ready for the eastbound. He liked keeping the teams together by color. That made it easier to remember which four needed resting and which were ready for the trail once again.

"You're getting to be almost enough of a hand to keep around this place," Ev said when Martin had brought the last of the horses to the corral.

"That mean I get a boost in my pay?"

"Once the note's retired, Martin."

"I'll likely have gray hairs by then," the boy grumbled. But the smile on his face betrayed a truer emotion.

Ev Raymond shielded his eyes from the bright midafternoon sun and gazed across the eastern horizon as a swirl of dust on the flat plain signaled the appearance of the westbound stage.

"Stage's comin'," Finley said, pointing to the dust.

Ev pulled a bright silver-plated watch from the small pocket of his trousers and read the time.

"On the mark today," Martin noted, stealing a glance at the watch. "Guess maybe I'd best warn Ma."

"Give her a hand with that stove wood, son," Ev suggested.

"Yes, sir," Martin answered, heading for the kitchen at the back of the house.

Ev closed the watch's cover and read the thin words etched there:

To Marshal Everett Raymond for ten years service.
The townspeople of Jacksboro had presented that watch to him only two years ago now, but it seemed more like

twenty. A lifetime had passed since Ev Raymond had surrendered the five-pointed star of town marshal.

By the time Martin had helped his mother light the stove fires and rejoined his father, the stagecoach had slowed for the ascent up Calvary Hill to the station.

So, they've met the schedule for once, Ev thought when old Art Hyland eased the coach to a halt beside the stable doors. Martin took the leaders from Art's pudgy fingers, and Ev unlatched the lefthand door so the passengers could step outside.

"We'll stop for dinner, folks," Art called out as he clumsily climbed down from the driver's roost.

As it happened, there were only two passengers aboard the stage. The first was Maude Magruder of Albany, on her way back from visiting a sick sister in Ft. Worth. The other was a young, sandy-haired stranger in his early twenties.

"I'm Rip Hazlewood," the young man said, extending a dusty right hand to Ev. "Know a place hereabouts where a man can put up for a few days?"

"Around here?" Martin asked, his bright blue eyes fixed on the stranger.

"Not much occasion for visitors here," Ev said, eyeing Hazlewood suspiciously. "Have family nearby?"

"No," he admitted.

"You look a little familiar," Ev said, examining the young man's face with care. "Been through here recently?"

"No, never."

"Would seem peculiar for a man to stay in a place he'd never been before, where he's got no family, no business."

"Didn't tell you I had no business here," Hazlewood replied with ease, shifting his weight to his heels. "Truth is I'm meeting some people, cousins of mine. They've been working cattle on some ranch south of here. I got a telegram they'd meet me at Antelope Springs sometime this week."

"Well, you're at the right place, no doubtin' that," Art confirmed.

"There's an eastbound stage due day after tomorrow," Martin said as he began unhitching the horses.

"That's my coach, bound back for Ft. Worth," Art said. "I could pass on a message for you."

"No need," Hazlewood said to Art. "I wired 'em back." He turned to Ev and said, "Now, you wouldn't be in a position to sell me three horses, would you? We plan on ridin' north from here."

"It'd make more sense to stay on the stage to Albany, then head out from there," Ev told the young man. "Cavalry at Ft. Griffin's got a fair road north into the Nations. There's a hotel now at the Flat, little town that's sprung up from the buffalo hunters' business."

"This suits our purposes better," Hazlewood explained. "Now, as to the horses. . ."

"We've got some good ones," Martin said, pointing toward the far corral.

"Mind if I have a look, Mr. . . . ."

"Raymond," Ev said, stepping aside so the newcomer could pass. "Everett Raymond. Dinner'll be ready shortly, though."

"I can smell it now," Hazlewood said. "Won't take me long. Anyway, I need to stretch a bit after ridin' bent in two inside that coach."

Ev nodded, then watched warily as Hazlewood stepped toward the distant corral. There wasn't time to watch closely, though, because Ev and Martin needed to release the weary horses from their harness. Fin and little Todd would lead the exhausted animals to the stable, then tend their needs. Besides giving each horse its feed and water, the youngsters would brush the animals' coats and examine the shoes.

Ev reserved for himself and Martin the more difficult task of bringing the fresh horses out of the ready corral and hitching them to the coach. Occasionally one of the animals would object to being strapped into place. More than once Ev had received a fair-sized bite or dodged an angry hoof. A short slap on the flank would usually quell such disturbances. Ev relied less on the whip, though, than on a firm hand on the leaders.

"We'll have a time of it in a couple of days when both stages get here at the same time," Martin said as they forced the horses into their places and secured the harness.

"Oh, one or the other's bound to be late," Ev said, amused. "It's always that way. I only remember one time when they both arrived within the same hour."

"How will we manage it?"

"Get the drivers to pitch in. Your ma can fix 'em a little somethin' special as our part of the bargain."

"Pa," Martin said, leaning against the coach and brushing back strands of thick, reddish-brown hair from his forehead. "You figure we'll ever get to ride one of these stages our own selves?"

"Oh, I've pretty much seen all of this world I need to see, Marty," Ev said, scratching his chin. "You, though, might buy yourself a ticket one of these days, head up to Wichita, and visit your ma's folks."

"Tom Shipley says they're building a railroad down south a ways."

"That'll likely put us out of business here. But there'll always be a market for horses."

"And a need for water."

"Now that'd be a thought, wouldn't it? We might find ourselves operatin' a railroad station."

"Might be a whole town here."

"Your ma wouldn't take to that. Lord, no, she'd raise Cain about us bein' in a town, that's for sure."

"How come she doesn't like towns, Pa?"

"Oh, I don't know that she doesn't. It's what comes with the towns that bothers her."

"What's that?" Martin asked, leaning against his father's shoulder.

"People—especially the kind that shoot guns off Sunday mornings or build saloons and bawdy houses."

"Like in Jacksboro."

"Like there and lots of other places."

"But I thought we had a good life in Jacksboro. She's always complainin' how there's no school for us here. We had a good school in Jacksboro."

"Well, I suspect it's like most things," Ev said, stepping away from Martin and tightening the harness. He then tied the leaders to the coach's brake. "There's good and bad to it. You tolerate the bad in order to enjoy the good."

"You like it here, Pa?"

"Sure, son," Ev said. He took Martin by the arm and pulled the sweaty fourteen-year-old along toward the house. "I have my work, my home, and my family. I can count on one hand the number of times I spent a whole month with your ma and you kids back in Jacksboro. There was always one feud or another to settle, some renegade soldier on the prowl, or else a man with an eye for easy money. Kept me busy, yes, sir."

After pausing at the basin long enough to wash their hands and faces, Ev and Martin joined the rest of the family in the dining room. Finley and Todd were sitting on either side of their little sister Rachel. On the opposite side of the table were Art Hyland and Mrs. Magruder. Ev nodded to his wife, Susan, then glanced back at the door for some sign of Hazlewood. There was none. Just as Ev was about to go search for the young man, Hazlewood stepped into the house from the back.

"Ah, you're here finally, Mr. Hazlewood," Susan said,

motioning to the vacant chair beside Art. "We may begin now."

Art reached for a roll, but Mrs. Magruder cleared her throat. The driver's bearlike hand retreated, and Susan's scowl vanished. They all bowed their heads, and Susan spoke a brief frontier prayer.

"For all God's bounty and grace, let us give heartfelt thanks. Amen."

Susan started the platters of food around. Beef, potatoes, carrots, and all sorts of greens were spooned onto plates. Fresh-baked squares of cornbread soaked up generous slices of butter. There was food enough to satisfy a regiment.

Sometimes I think that's what I'm raising here, Ev thought as he watched Martin dip a corner of cornbread into beef gravy, then stuff it into his mouth. Fin and Todd weren't a lot better, gobbling food as if they hadn't been fed in a month of Sundays. Even little Rachel, yet to celebrate her seventh birthday, chomped alway at a carrot.

"It's what we get for raising them in boarding houses and way stations," Susan had often complained.

Ev usually laughed her complaints away. The children, if a little wild, were cut from that self-reliant mold found more often than not along the frontier. And if the boys didn't have their hair cut as often as they might, and Rachel lagged behind on her verses three Sundays out of four, they never backed away from chores.

"You must have had a full garden this year, Susan," Maude Magruder remarked as the last carrot disappeared.

"The rains were generous," Susan said.

"And, of course, you've the water from the springs," Maude commented. "My, my sister Emily would certainly swap her place for yours. Water year-around! You're truly blessed."

"Yes, we are," Susan said, holding back a smile. She'd often remarked that Maude Magruder could talk the hide off a mule.

"Get a lot of visitors through here?" Hazlewood asked.

"Not many," Ev said.

"Almost never overnight," Art said. He rocked back in his chair so that his expanded girth might have a little more room. "Not much around here 'cept a few ranches. Merritt place beyond Calvary Hill, and the old Keller farm past that. Kellers haven't been there since Quannah Parker burned their barn. . . back when, Ev, '72?"

"Might've been," Ev said. "We weren't here then, remember?"

"Pa was still marshal of Jacksboro in '72," Martin said proudly.

"That right?" Hazlewood asked, his tight lips forming into a smile. "You a marshal?"

"Was," Ev said, avoiding Hazlewood's eyes. "Now I'm just an honest innkeeper."

Finley whispered something to Todd, who laughed. Those two, with their bright eyes and yellow hair, put Ev constantly in mind of their mother—those laughing eyes of hers could still bedevil him.

"I noticed those two Winchesters over your fireplace," Hazlewood said, breaking the spell Ev'd fallen under. "Don't suppose you have a lot of use for them?"

"Not the fireplace anyway," Susan answered. "Now and then, Ev does a little hunting."

"Much game hereabouts?" Hazlewood asked.

"Deer in the fall, out in the thickets," Ev said, chewing the last bite of his potato. "Bobwhite, ducks in early winter. Sometimes we shoot a prowlin' wolf."

"Not much excitement compared to a town like Jacksboro," Hazlewood said, smiling. "Miss it?"

"No," Susan said. She glanced nervously at her husband.

"You know Jacksboro?" Ev asked, searching his memory for some clue as to where he'd seen Hazlewood's face. The cut of the stranger's jaw, the mischief in the eyes. . . Ev'd seen them before. He was certain of it.

"Can't say I have," Hazlewood told them. "I hear it's a good market for stock, though."

"You interested in stock, are you?" Art asked. "I've got a brother down in. . ."

"Watch he doesn't sell you a lame donkey for a Kentucky thoroughbred," Ev joked. "Art's brother Tom'd trade you out of your drawers if given half a chance."

The table rocked with laughter, and even Art joined in. Susan stood up then and motioned to the children. Rachel and Todd began removing the dishes.

"A fine meal, Mrs. Raymond," Hazlewood said, rising from his place. "Fine indeed."

"Can we get you anything else, Mr. Hazlewood?" Ev asked.

"Nothing else to eat, thank you, but I could use a hand getting my chest off the stage."

Ev glanced at Art, but the driver seemed in no hurry to move, much less offer help with the chest.

"Fine," Ev said. He started for the door. "Let's get it. Afterward I'll show you the guest room."

"We'll be on the road again soon, no doubt," Mrs. Magruder said, her voice betraying a touch of regret. "Is there somewhere I might refresh myself?"

"I'll show you," Susan said. "Just follow me, Maude."

As the ladies headed out the back door, Ev led the way to the coach. Minutes later he and Rip Hazlewood removed a large trunk from the luggage boot.

"You plan on quite a stay?" Ev asked as they lugged the chest to the guest quarters behind the dining room.

"Two, maybe three days."

Ev pointed to a bare bed, and little Rachel arrived with some bedding.

"It's a dollar a day for bed, four bits for board," Ev explained.

"How much for the mustang with the black feet?"

"The stallion? He's not fully broke to saddle."

"He appeared gentle enough. For me. I'll bend him to my needs as we get acquainted. I'm not lookin' for an old mare or a gelding."

"Suit yourself, Hazlewood. I planned on getting twenty, thirty dollars for him at Weatherford."

"I know a good pony when I see one," Hazlewood said. He pulled from his pocket a roll of crisp greenbacks and peeled three bills off the top. "Here's the thirty. And ten more if you've got a saddle."

"Best I can do's an old army saddle. It's been mended. I wouldn't give a man ten dollars for it myself."

"Say I'm in a generous mood."

"Looks as though you can afford to be," Ev said, staring at the bank notes.

"Had a lucky day at the card table. Plan on buyin' into a ranch up on the Trinity. That's why I'm meetin' my cousins. I'll need a pair of mounts for them, too."

"We'll tend to that when they arrive. And I'd use caution showing that much money to anyone," Ev said. "Men've been killed up at the Flats for less than fifty dollars."

"But not by a man with a pretty wife and four kids," Hazlewood said, smiling broadly. "No, I'd say I'm safe as a newborn babe here."

Newborn babes have a bad habit of dying on the Texas frontier, Ev thought as he left Hazlewood in the room alone and headed back to his chores. He wanted to work the stallion with the dark feet once before turning him over to Hazlewood, and the two spotted ponies might do for the others.

I wish I could remember where I've seen that face, Ev mused as he crossed the road and approached the corral.

Was he one of the gamblers at the Lost Creek Saloon? Or could he be one of the cowboys who drifted through town on their way home from driving cows to Kansas?

Ev frowned. There was also a darker possibility, one that troubled him. Maybe he'd seen that face on a poster. It wasn't likely, Hazlewood being so young and all. But that didn't help Ev breathe any easier.

CHAPTER 2

THERE was nothing about Rip Hazlewood's actions those next two days that hinted he was anything other than what he said, a young cowboy awaiting the arrival of his cousins so that they could ride north and buy a ranch up on the Trinity. And even though it seemed strange to Ev that Hazlewood should meet anyone at Antelope Springs in order to ride all the way back to the Trinity, that didn't mean it wasn't true.

"It's all that time spent as a marshal," Susan told him. "You just can't take a man at face value anymore. Look at the shine Marty's taken to him. Ever know that boy to read a man wrong?"

No, Ev had to agree. Martin wasn't easily fooled. And the truth was that Martin hung on Hazlewood's every word, followed him all over the ranch. To Hazlewood's credit, he pitched in with the chores: he helped Fin and Todd paint the stable, and joined Rachel at hanging out washing.

Clearly, Martin was impressed by the stranger. "He's a good hand with horses," Martin said to his father. "Told me he grew up breaking mustangs down on the Colorado River."

"Carries a lot of gear for a wayfarer," Ev pointed out.

"Most of it belonged to his father, Pa. He picked up that trunk in Ft. Worth. It's been in an old warehouse."

"I suppose that's possible," Ev grumbled.

But there was little enough time in a day to get all the work done, and with two stages due in the following morning and all the cattle needing to be moved to fresh pasture, there wasn't a moment to be spared for checking out Hazlewood's background or plans.

After all, Ev told himself, what profit would there be in robbing us? The forty dollars Hazlewood himself had handed over constituted all but a few dollars of the Raymonds' cash. It didn't seem worthwhile to ride all the way to Antelope Springs to steal a few ponies.

No, there's nothing here a man would find worth taking, Ev thought. Lots of heat and sweat and hard work. That was about all.

Ev swept the whole subject out of his mind as he sent Todd to slap paint on the last bare wall of the stable. Susan and Rachel were digging vegetables out of the garden. Rip Hazelwood devoted his energies to working with the black-footed stallion, as Finley and Martin looked on.

"It's time to move the cows," Ev announced to the two boys.

"Can't we stay and watch Rip ride the stallion?" Martin asked. "Just a little while?"

"No such thing as a little while," Ev said, pointing to the waiting horses.

"I know, Pa," Martin said, sighing. "Was just a thought."

Finley didn't say a word, just pulled himself onto a pony. Ev mounted the big brown stallion and led the way toward the far pasture. Before he was fifty yards past the barn, Martin had joined them.

In the next two hours they nudged three hundred longhorns over a hill and down into a grassy stretch of bottomland near Carson Creek. There wasn't any creek in the summer, just a series of mudholes. But enough water collected at some points to satisfy the cattle. When the work was finished, Ev raced the boys back as far as the pond. The three of them then tied their horses and dove headfirst into the cooling waters.

"Glad you thought of this, Pa," Martin said. He stripped off his soggy shirt and tossed it to the bank. "I didn't think we'd ever get Fin another bath. Todd and I were afraid all that new paint we put on the barn might peel off next time he walked by."

"You're not so sweet smelling your own self, Marty Raymond," Finley said, splashing water at his brother. It was a mistake. In a flash Martin was charging through the shallows, shoving mountains of water in Finley's direction. Then, with a war whoop, Martin pushed his brother's surprised head underwater.

Rachel, who was standing atop the hill watching, squealed with delight, and soon Susan appeared as well, hands on her hips in pretended anger. Ev read the brightness in her azure eyes as a sign the foolishness would be tolerated a little longer.

"Don't altogether drown him," Ev said from the safety of the far end of the pond. "He's gotten to where he does a fair job of grooming a horse."

"I suppose," Martin said, releasing Finley at last. "But I do figure he's goin' to have a bath."

In spite of poor Finley's protests, Martin managed to remove the boy's clothing. Susan brought down a cake of soap, along with an equally unhappy Todd.

"This is worse'n an Indian attack," Finley complained as Ev scrubbed soap into the boy's flaxen-blond hair. "You'd think a body who's twelve is old enough to take his own bath."

"You would, wouldn't you?" Susan said gleefully.

While the boys washed dirt and sweat from their tanned shoulders, Susan dragged Rachel back to the house. It was near time for dinner, and there were as many chores inside a house as there were outside.

"How come I can't have my bath in the waterhole?" the little girl shouted.

"Because young ladies are not bred to the habits of hooligans and cowboys," her mother explained.

Ev couldn't help chuckling.

"They'll spend half a mornin' heatin' water and fillin' a tub in the kitchen," Todd grumbled. "That means choppin' a mountain of wood!"

"Seems a small enough price to pay for your ma's cookin'," Rip Hazlewood said, stepping to the edge of the pond. "Is this a private bath, or can any old cowboy join in?"

Ev laughed, and Martin motioned Hazlewood on. Soon the young visitor was shed of his clothes and in the water.

"Feels good to be alive again," Hazlewood said, plunging a weary head under the water. "Gets hot nowadays, doesn't it?"

"Sure does," Martin agreed, splashing over beside Hazlewood. The two of them were soon laughing and occasionally splashing each other.

It surprised Ev. Martin hadn't acted so much like a boy in a year and a half. But that wasn't everything Ev observed. For a cowboy, Hazlewood's shoulders were remarkably pale, whiter than one of Susan's clean sheets. There were a pair of scars on one shoulder, too, the thin, red kind Ev remembered so well from the war. They were usually made by minie balls. One didn't appear to be more than a year healed.

"I see you noticed my medals, Mr. Raymond," Hazlewood said, appearing a little nervous for the first time. "Got myself shot a couple of times."

"Shot?" Todd asked, splashing over to have a look.

"How'd that happen?" Martin asked, studying the scars.

"I was trailin' old Doc Mangus's herd up to Abilene."

"Abilene?" Ev asked. "Must've been a long time ago. Nobody's trailed cattle into Abilene since what, '71?"

"I was fifteen, on my first drive," Hazlewood continued. "Out of the sun came a bunch of rustlers, ridin' and shootin' and yellin' so I thought the world was endin'. Why, I didn't even have myself a pistol. They shot me there, twice, took my gear, my horse, even my boots. If it hadn't been for ol'd Doc findin' me, I'd be dead today."

Ev thought to say something, but the glow in Martin's eyes stopped him. So what if Hazlewood was lying? What did it matter? More likely he'd cheated some poor farmer at cards and caught a bullet for his trouble. It bothered Ev that both shots seemed to have come from the back. Men usually got shot that way when they ran from someone. But then there was the other possibility that Hazlewood had been ambushed.

"I see you've caught a ball or two in your time, too," Hazlewood said, gazing over at Ev.

"Pa was in the cavalry," Fin said proudly. "With Forrest up in Tennessee, then down in Mississippi and Alabama."

"Proud to know you, indeed I am," Hazlewood said, his easy manner fully restored as he shook Ev's hand. "My own pa served in Virginia, in Hood's brigade. Got himself bayonetted at Sharpsburg. My brother Haskell, too, the same day."

"Who brought you up?" Ev asked, softening a bit as he read the sadness in Hazlewood's eyes.

"My Uncle George," Hazlewood said, rinsing the last spot of lather from his arms. "Taught me all I know. He's a fine man."

"I'm sure he is," Ev said, pulling Todd over so an inspection could be made of the boy's ears. A little more scrubbing was required to insure Todd would pass his mother's muster. Finley's neck merited additional attention as well. When everyone was tolerably clean, Ev waved them to the bank. Soon they were dressed and busy leading the horses back to the corral.

"Umm. . . Fresh bread for supper," Fin announced as they unsaddled the mounts.

"In your honor, Mr. Hazlewood," Ev pointed out.

"It's about time you folks started callin' me Rip," Hazlewood declared.

"Sure, Rip," Martin said.

"Will you tell us some more stories about Kansas and the cattle trails and all?" Todd asked.

"Oh, I expect your pa's got more interestin' tales to spin, him servin' with Forrest in the war."

"He never tells us anything," Martin explained. "All we ever talk about's horses and cows."

"Less excitin' than shootouts with rustlers, I suppose," Ev said.

Hazlewood smiled and said, "Well, Mr. Raymond, you remember bein' young."

Sure, Ev thought as he lifted the heavy saddle from his horse's back. Boys would have their stories.

And Rip Hazlewood never seemed to tire of spinning tales. All through dinner and half an hour afterward Hazlewood told of adventures in Dodge City and Abilene. Finally Ev helped Susan clear the table. Then the two of them stepped outside, leaving Hazlewood with the children.

"They've about adopted him into the family," Susan said, taking Ev's hand and leading him off toward the rim of Calvary Hill.

"Seems like it," Ev said.

"Does it worry you?"

"Don't see how it should."

"That's not what I asked, Ev. It does, doesn't it?"

"Yes."

"Then you should send him on his way. There's no law that says we have to house just anyone here."

"I can't send a man packin' for no reason. Especially when Martin's gotten so close to him."

"He's quite a storyteller. You don't think he's got cousins at all, do you?"

"Oh, it's not his stories, Susan," Ev said, glancing off at the distant sunset.

"Then what?"

"I've seen him somewhere before. I can't remember where, but I know that face."

"He could be an outlaw, then."

"More likely just a gambler. I've run across a lot of men."

"It's possible you might have forgotten where you ran across him, Ev, but it's less likely he wouldn't remember you. People don't forget a man who's marshal of a town like Jacksboro."

"I could be mistaken."

"Oh? How many times have you been wrong about a face? I can't think of a single one."

"He wouldn't be apt to step forward and tell me he was a cowboy I locked up for being drunk or a gambler I had to chase out of the county."

"Or a man with his picture on a wanted poster."

"Yes, there's that, too."

"So what do we do?"

"I don't know that we do anything, Susan. He hasn't done anything wrong. Truth is, he's helped some. It'd be easier if he'd made threats, been rough with the children. But he hasn't. Still, I think I'll have a look at some of the posters."

"You still have some?"

"Boxed in the loft, along with some other relics."

"Your cavalry sabre?"

"Probably he'll be gone tomorrow at any rate. Art comes back through in the mornin' with the eastbound stage. If Hazlewood's cousins aren't aboard, I'll send a letter to Mitch Burnett at Brazos Crossing, tell him to ask around."

"And if you find out he's wanted?"

"I guess we'll see if I've really put Jacksboro behind me."

"Do you still miss it?" Susan asked, holding his arm tightly.

"Sometimes," Ev told her. "I always felt like I was doing

important work in Jacksboro, keeping the peace, looking after those who couldn't take care of themselves."

"And now?"

"What do we do here, run a few horses, raise some cattle?"

"We survive, Ev."

"I know. Whatever else I miss, I don't regret quittin'. The killin' gets to you, makes you hard. I remember the long nights off on some hillside all alone, wonderin' what tomorrow would bring, not knowin' if there'd be a next week. Now when I'm workin' with Martin down at the corral or scrubbin' Todd's neck or seein' to it Rachel's tucked in at night, I know I'm where I need to be." He squeezed her hand. "The best times are when we're out here on this hillside, Susan, sharin' the quiet hours we stumble onto now and again."

"I don't miss Jacksboro, Ev. See, I remember those long nights, too. They were an eternity for me. I never slept. And it was hard for the children. Rachel and Todd used to wake with nightmares. Finley would crawl into a corner and sort of moan. Only Martin was old enough to understand. And I guess he was too busy being the oldest to worry."

"You did a fine job with them all. I know I wasn't much help."

"You're doing your part now."

Ev drew her nearer, and he felt that closeness that was most of all missing on those dark nights in the Jack County hills, waiting for some outlaw or band of cattle thieves.

Later that night, when the sun had died in the western hills, Ev and Susan stood together in the hallway, watching moonbeams dance across Rachel's forehead. Then they stepped to the next door and looked in on the boys.

Todd and Finley were lying dead to the world on their simple beds, their hair blending in with loose straw. Martin was curled up near the far wall beneath the open window. Susan stepped inside long enough to pull a sheet over his chest. Her light footsteps were hardly audible over the loud chirping of the crickets outside.

"The whole world seems at peace," she whispered to Ev after she returned to the hall.

"Yes."

As he led her to the corner bedroom they shared, he remembered the posters in the loft. But it was late, and tomorrow would be a long day. Besides, what difference could it make?

CHAPTER 3

DAWN broke over the eastern hills, casting a golden tint upon the land. Grotesque shadows were cast from the misshapen branches of the live oaks beyond the stable, and an eerie silence seemed to possess the place.

Days started early at Antelope Springs, especially when two stages were due at the station. Already Martin and Finley were busy tending the livestock. Soon little Todd would be gathering eggs from the chicken coop. Rachel could be detected carrying wood from the kindling box to the kitchen so her mother could light the stove and start breakfast.

Ev greeted the morning as he always did, yawning away the weariness that came with working the land in summer. He pulled on a blue shirt of homespun cotton and some denim trousers, then stumbled outside to check on the work.

"Good mornin', Pa," Finley said, leading a brown mare out of the stable to the ready corral. The boy's bare, tanned shoulders were swallowed by a pair of Martin's old overalls. Hazlewood stood in the yard watching.

"Mornin', son," Ev replied, forcing a smile onto his face as answer to Finley's bright blue eyes.

"Red sky," Finley pointed out. "Maybe we'll get some rain."

"Likely," Ev agreed, staring at the heavens. Finley was right. There were clouds across the whole western quarter of the sky. The sun blazed through them, painting the land below with splashes of scarlet.

Blood red, Ev thought, just like the morning after Selma

when it seemed nothing would ever wash away the smell of smoke and death from the landscape. His hands trembled as he recalled the horror of that battle, the terrible taste of defeat that had filled them all. But the war was over now. Ev faced only another difficult day of work, not a Union army bent on destroying Forrest's cavalry.

"Gettin' an early jump on the day's work, huh?" Rip Hazlewood asked then, jolting Ev from his trance.

"Best way," Ev replied, waving Finley by with another horse.

"Guess it must get a little busy 'round here when you've got both stages comin' through the same day."

"Usually," Ev said, frowning. "How'd you know both coaches were comin' in today?"

"You must've told me," Hazlewood said. He shrugged. "Or maybe it was Martin."

"Your cousins might be on the eastbound."

"Could be. They sometimes drag their feet, though. I wouldn't be surprised if they took a little longer."

"You might ride on along to Albany, see if they could be waitin' there."

"No, I'm satisfied to wait here."

A smile spread across Hazlewood's face. It seemed to Ev the stranger would be just as pleased if his cousins didn't arrive. For a moment Ev considered insisting Hazlewood board the westbound if the cousins didn't appear. But when Martin trotted over to show off his handling of the horses, Ev knew it wouldn't do. No, unless some good reason could be found to send Hazlewood packing, he'd have to be tolerated a bit longer. But it wouldn't hurt to send word on to Mitch Burnett.

"I guess the eastbound usually pulls in first," Hazlewood said, scanning the western horizon for some hint of the stagecoach.

"Most of the time," Ev told him.

"Don't suppose it carries a lot of passengers."

"Depends," Ev said, eyeing Hazlewood suspiciously. "You seem awfully curious this morning."

"Oh, just passin' the time, Mr. Raymond. I got to thinkin' how maybe my cousins might not be able to buy a seat if the stage was full."

"Can't recall a time when there wasn't a seat to be had eastbound. Sometimes the westbound coach is booked."

"It's strange there'd be more folks headed out to this place than away."

"I don't know. It's a good enough place. We have water from the springs, even in the heart of summer. The stock have good grass. Sometimes I see wild mustangs off in the hills. I've roped more than a few of 'em, broke 'em to saddle. . ."

"Seems a hard life."

"Oh, I wouldn't say it isn't, but the hardness of a place is what makes it worth taming. I remember riding through places along the Mississippi that looked like they belonged in a story book. The fields were so green you wanted to taste them. But it didn't seem to me the people there were particularly strong. To survive in a place like this, all off away from anybody, you have to rely on yourself. I want my boys to learn to fend for themselves, to get by on what they grow from the earth, on what they earn from a hard day's labor."

"Must get terribly lonely sometimes."

"Well, we don't have many neighbors," Ev admitted. "But it's my place, and there's comfort in knowing you have a place to belong to. There's lots of room to spread out onto, to grow. Isn't that what you and your cousins are lookin' for?"

"Maybe," Hazlewood said, gazing off across the rolling hills toward the far horizon. "Mostly I'm tired of bein' just another. . ."

"Just another what?" Ev asked, waiting for Hazlewood to finish.

"Face," Hazlewood said, trembling slightly as he turned to stare intently into Ev's eyes. "See, no one ever remembers somebody like me. But they will."

Hazlewood spoke with a certainty that chilled Ev. He'd heard such boasting before, on the streets and in the saloons of Jacksboro. But Hazlewood didn't dwell on the subject, and there was too much work to be done for Ev to devote any extra time to wondering about it.

Martin and Finley had fed the stock and brought the relief team to the ready corral when Susan called out that breakfast was ready. After stopping at the wash basin to scrub hands, Ev and the boys took their accustomed places around the table while Susan set platters of hot eggs and sausage alongside a dutch oven full of fresh biscuits.

"Puts me in mind of my mama's cookin'," Hazlewood said as he chewed a biscuit.

"Did you grow up on a ranch, too, Rip?" Martin asked.

"No, we moved around a lot," Hazlewood explained. "Mama used to cook for folks. At ranches, roomin' houses, hotels, even once at a way station like this one."

"Where is she now?" Susan asked.

"Oh, she's gone on to her reward, ma'am," Hazlewood said, his eyes darkening. "I suppose it was a relief to her to have her trials over. We never had more'n a few dollars at any one time. Mostly we owed everyone we knew."

"I recall you sayin' your pa is dead," Ev said.

"The war, Mr. Raymond," Hazlewood said. "Was with Hood in the East."

Hazlewood told a dozen tales of his father's adventures in the war over breakfast. When everyone had finished eating and the last story had concluded, Ev assigned Fin to clear the table and allowed Martin, Todd, and Rachel to go fishing down at the pond.

"I imagine Martin can find you a pole," Ev said to Hazlewood. "This time of year the perch bite fair this hour of the day."

"Think I'd rather wait out the stage," Hazlewood replied. "Shouldn't be too much longer."

"I never go predictin' arrival times, not on this line. One week the stage is right on the mark. Next time around, it may be three days behind schedule. Roads get washed out, and horses throw shoes. Drivers get sick. Couple of months back a pair of renegade drovers shot the westbound driver, took the mailbag and close to a thousand dollars off the passengers. Then they took off with the team, leavin' the people to walk more than thirty miles."

"Ever catch up with the outlaws?"

"Found 'em three days later, holed up in a bawdy house up near the Flat. Two rangers went in and killed 'em. Most of the money was recovered."

"Martin says you served some time as a peace officer. You help with the trackin'?"

"No, I've retired from the law. I keep busy mindin' my own business, which just now is mendin' a harness, not gabbin' all day with Rip Hazlewood."

"Don't let me keep you from your work."

"I won't," Ev said, heading for the stable.

Ev devoted better than an hour to repairing torn bits of leather harness that would be needed by the westbound team. By the time the job was finished, the boys had tired of fishing. Instead they spread out piles of hay on the barn floor and jumped from the loft, laughing and shouting as they plunged to the ground and rolled in the straw. From time to time Todd and Fin would jump on Martin, tormenting their older brother with scratchy straws. Marty would put up with it only so long. Then the dark-haired boy would grab a skinny brother in each arm and drag them through the straw until Finley and Todd had about as much hay in their overalls as they had boy. Ev occasionally scolded the three if things threatened to get out of hand. Otherwise, he merely grinned and recalled the day when he himself might have been in the middle of it.

"Oughtn't somebody keep watch for the stage?" Hazlewood asked as Ev satisfied himself the harness would hold.

"Oh, they'll let us know when they get here," Ev assured him.

"But hadn't you best get ready for it?"

"We've done what's needed," Ev said. "No need to worry. Susan's bakin' extra bread, and the horses are ready. Why don't you take a turn at the hay?"

"I've outgrown boys' games," Hazlewood said, a bit irritated. "I've got more important concerns."

"Well, be patient. The coach should be along soon."

But nothing Ev said seemed to have any effect on Rip Hazlewood. The young man paced back and forth across the barn, complaining about worthless schedules and undependable stage lines.

"You'd think he had a bride on that coach," Ev joked.

Even Martin seemed unnerved by Hazlewood's suddenly jittery behavior. It wasn't until the heavy pounding of the stage's four wheels could be heard echoing across the valley below that Hazlewood regained his composure.

"It's the eastbound, all right, Pa," Martin declared as the stage got closer.

But now, at the moment Hazlewood had been awaiting, Hazlewood himself could not be found.

"Where's Rip?" Martin called out from the door of the barn.

"That's not our main concern just this moment," Ev said, waving the boys toward the ready corral. "Time to exchange the teams."

Martin nodded and headed for the corral. Finley and Todd followed. Rachel and Susan were busy inside the house, preparing dinner for the passengers.

"Welcome to Antelope Springs," Ev said as the coach pulled into the station. "My wife's readyin' food."

"I could use a little something in my gullet," Art Hyland said, rubbing his generous stomach.

Ev nodded to Art, then opened the coach door. Two men stepped out. The first was of a type Ev knew all too well.

"Gambler," Ev mumbled, noticing the pearl cufflinks and the shiny buttons on the man's coat.

The other dressed like a drover, but there was something about the man's youthful smile that betrayed him.

"This is my cousin, Buck Wood," Hazlewood told them as he reappeared. "He's come to share my good fortune."

"That's right," Buck said, stepping down from the coach. "I'm here to enjoy all that can be had."

The young man examined every inch of the barnyard, then started for the house.

"Hold up there a moment," Ev said. "My wife will call when the food's ready."

"Oh, I don't know about waitin'," Buck said. "I've got my own schedule, so to speak. Right, Rip?"

It was only then that Ev spotted the riders, two solitary figures on horseback edging out of the shadows of the live oaks toward Antelope Springs.

"Pa?" Finley asked, pointing to the first, a burly figure holding a rifle across one knee.

"Art, we've got company," Ev said, nodding toward the two approaching horsemen.

"I see 'em," Art said, clumsily feeling around the coach for the rifle he kept hidden there.

"Martin, Fin, Todd, get inside the house!" Ev shouted.

The boys scrambled toward the door as the gambler drew a pistol from his coat pocket and swung it in the direction of the riders.

"I can't find. . ." Art Hyland began. He never finished. An earshattering blast from the edge of the porch drowned the words. The gambler dropped to one knee, then crumbled like a dry leaf in autumn.

"What the. . ." Ev said as young Buck Wood stepped down from the porch holding Art's misplaced Winchester. A thin plume of smoke rose from the tip of the barrel.

"Nothin' to concern yourself with," Hazlewood said as Buck led Art away. "Just do as you're told, and nobody'll get hurt."

Ev glanced at his Sharps carbine near the door. But the feel of a Winchester in his back erased all thought of making a dash for it.

"Waitin' for cousins, huh?" Ev asked as he stared over his shoulder at Hazlewood's grinning face.

"These are my cousins," Hazlewood explained. "Buck Wood you've met. His brother Ben's yonder, together with our Uncle George."

"George?" Ev said, glaring at Hazlewood's laughing eyes, then examining the heavyset figure growing nearer.

"George Nolan."

"I remember now," Ev said, choking on the words. "You boys and your uncle robbed old Mrs. Jacklin of her savings. I shot your partner, Luke Royal."

"Wasn't much of a loss, if you ask me," Hazlewood joked.

Ev frowned as he remembered the incident. There was Hazlewood, no more than twenty, doing his uncle's bidding by getting someone drunk, then stealing his cash. Only Mrs. Jacklin declined to play the game. Nolan had killed her.

"You remember now, don't you?" Hazlewood said, smiling. "That's good. It makes the next part easier."

"And what would that be, robbin' my boys of their boots?"

"Not enough money to it. Thanks just the same. No, we're here to do what nobody's ever tried. We're robbin' both the eastbound and westbound stages."

"Oh, Lord," Ev muttered as he digested the news. The eastbound rarely carried so much as twenty dollars. The westbound would bring along payrolls for the three biggest ranches in the vicinity.

"I remember you, too, Marshal," Hazlewood said as Ev stepped back from the coach. "Don't you get any ideas of turnin' things to your favor."

"Just you see my wife and family aren't bothered."

"That'll be largely up to you," a deeper voice announced from five yards away.

"Nolan," Ev said, gazing bitterly into the outlaw's eyes.

"That's right, Marshal," Nolan said, climbing down from his horse. "I see you've met young Rip. I knew you two'd get on. Now, I believe we've got a score to settle."

Ev glanced at the porch where the Sharps rested untouched. Martin and Finley stared out the front window, their eyes full of fear. Susan huddled with Todd and Rachel in the doorway.

"Listen to me, Nolan," Ev rasped, steadying his trembling fingers. "If any harm comes to my family, you'd best make good and sure I'm dead. Otherwise. . ."

"Oh, we'll tend to that in time," Buck interrupted. "Luke Royal was a friend of mine. One thing everyone knows about the Nolans is that we pay our debts."

Ev felt something inside himself die as Buck raised the Winchester.

"Not yet, boy," Nolan objected. "Everything in its own time."

Ev had no time to relax, though. Nolan turned quick as a cat and laid the blunt end of a long-barreled Colt across Ev's head. For a second Ev stared wide-eyed at the grinning outlaws. Then darkness swallowed his world.

CHAPTER 4

FOR close to an hour Ev drifted in and out of a world of shadows. Pain exploded through the back of his head, and his vision remained clouded. When the haze finally cleared, he found himself lying on the floor of the dining room, his head resting in Susan's lap. Sounds of splintered wood and breaking glass filled the air.

"Don't try to move around," Susan said as Ev tried to sit up. "It looks like you've got a tomato growing out of the back of your head."

"Does it hurt, Pa?" Finley asked.

Ev blinked away the pain and managed to muffle a moan. He glanced around the room, then frowned. The table was turned on its end, and plates were scattered about. The glass panels were smashed out of Susan's hutch, and the fine china cups that had belonged to her Norwegian grandmother lay in fragments on the floor.

"Yes, they've made a pretty big mess," Susan admitted, lightly stroking the side of his shoulder. "But so far no one's been hurt."

"Except that gambler," Ev said, remembering the shooting earlier.

"He's not dead," Fin said, crawling over beside Ev. "They took him and Art Hyland into the storeroom."

"The bullet went cleanly through his arm," Susan said. "I don't suppose he'll have much need for shuffling cards just now anyway."

"No," Ev agreed. "Help me sit up."

"It'd be better if you'd rest awhile."

Ev looked at the fearful eyes of the children and mustered his strength. No, just now they needed to see him up, in charge. So despite the ringing in his ears, he rolled to one side and, with Susan's help, managed to pull himself against the wall and sit up.

"Pa?" little Todd asked, slipping his head under Ev's arm and leaning against his father's chest.

"It's goin' to be all right," Ev said, pulling Finley over, too. Little Rachel burrowed her way between Ev and Susan. Only Martin remained apart, sitting five or six feet away, glaring angrily at some unseen terror beyond the room.

"He pretended to be our friend," Martin finally cried, tears of fury rolling down his cheeks. "And all the time he was plannin' to rob us! It's my fault."

"No," Ev said firmly, feeling the trembling hands of the other children. Susan cradled Rachel, and Ev found his left arm smothered by Todd's small hands.

"He lied, Pa," Martin said, rubbing his eyes. "I liked him."

"I know, son," Ev said. "He fooled us all. But now we know. We won't make the same mistake again."

"No," Martin agreed.

Ev beckoned Martin closer, and the boy reluctantly stepped over.

"What's done is done," Ev said, resting a heavy hand on Martin's shoulder. "That's over."

Martin nodded, but Ev read a mixture of guilt and fear in the boy's eyes. He wanted to say something to lift Martin's spirits, to ease the worries of the others, but before his lips could form a word, George Nolan charged into the room, laughing so that the ground seemed to shake.

"Well, the marshal's alive again," Nolan jeered. "Thought I might've hit you a little too hard. Wouldn't want you to miss our little party."

Ben and Buck Wood waltzed through the doorway, dressed in petticoats looted from Susan's cedar chest and waving stolen bottles of whiskey in the air.

"Don't you boys look pretty!" Nolan shouted, grabbing the bottle from Buck and taking a long sip. "All we need is a little music, and we could have ourselves a ball."

Ev reached over and took Susan's hand. Her face reddened as Ben and Buck ripped the delicate garments to shreds and tossed the remnants around the dining room.

"Oh, Ev," Susan cried, resting her head on his shoulder.

Ev felt her tears drop on his chest. It was as though all the treasures of a lifetime lay shattered and broken at their feet. But it wasn't just the torn petticoats and the broken cups that hammered away at Ev. It was not knowing what still lay ahead. Gazing into Nolan's bloodshot eyes, Ev couldn't help suspecting the worst was yet to come.

Rip Hazlewood entered the room, grinning as he handed his uncle a small white box.

"Oh, no," Susan mumbled.

Ev felt something inside himself sink as George Nolan opened the box. The gentle notes of an Irish lullaby drifted through the room. Susan's father had brought the box up from New Orleans for her wedding. That same song had always chased off the worst despair, had sung each of the children to sleep some restless night.

"Put it down!" Martin screamed, jumping to his feet. "That's my mother's! Put it down!"

"Well, what've we got here?" Nolan asked, stepping toward the boy.

"I said to put that down!" Martin yelled.

"Uncle George?" Hazlewood said, setting off to intercept Nolan.

"You best stay out of this, pup!" Nolan hollered to his nephew. "This is business I've got to settle with this cub of a marshal."

Ev eased away from Susan and shook loose of the boys. But though he tried his best, he couldn't manage to stand up. His head was full of cobwebs, and he fought to focus his eyes as Martin confronted Nolan.

"Give it to me," Martin said, the fear in his eyes changing to hatred. "You've got no right. . ."

"Right?" Nolan bellowed. "You want to hear about right, boys?"

The Wood brothers hooted, and Nolan set the whiskey bottle down on what was left of the hutch. Instead he slowly, calmly drew out a pistol and pointed it at Martin's face.

"Want to tell me about right, do you, cub?" Nolan asked. "In this land, the only man who's right is the one that's got the pistol in his hand."

The Woods hooted their agreement, and Ev heard Todd whimper. Rachel clutched her mother's side. But Finley released his grip on Ev's hand and slowly rose.

"Here's another one, Uncle George!" Ben said, waving his bottle in Finley's direction.

"They're just kids," Hazlewood pleaded.

"Sure, Rip, so we'll just play a game or two with 'em," Ben joshed as he took a long pull at the bottle, then tossed it to his brother. "You don't hold against us havin' ourselves a little fun, do you?"

"So, Marshal, what do you have to say about this?" Nolan asked, kicking a chair toward Ev. "You teach these boys to stand up for themselves? Isn't always the smartest thing to do."

Ev again fought to get to his feet. It wasn't possible, but he did manage to reach out and grab Finley's belt. Although Fin struggled to free himself, Ev pulled the boy back.

"Well, Marshal?" Nolan asked again.

"Can't you see he's only half-conscious?" Susan screamed.

"Or that's what he wants us to think," Nolan said, leering, "That right, Marshal? I hit you too hard?"

"Why don't you just go ahead and shoot, Nolan?" Ev asked, gritting his teeth. "You'll do it sooner or later."

"No, Uncle George," Hazlewood said, stepping between them. "The shots. Think about it. The other stage can't be far from here."

"Then why don't you go look out for it?" Nolan asked. "You're right, though. Why shoot him?"

Nolan replaced the revolver in its holster, then drew a large knife from a scabbard in his left boot. Finley shrank back, and Martin shuddered.

"Uncle George?" Hazlewood pleaded.

"Get outside, Rip! See he goes, Bucky!"

Nolan gestured wildly, and Buck Wood escorted Hazlewood from the room. Nolan examined the music box, then rewound the small key so that the music played a second time.

"It is pretty, Uncle George," Ben observed.

"Is it?" Nolan asked, turning to Susan and grinning cruelly. "I never took to pretty things. They belong in churches and fine houses. I don't care much for those, either!"

Nolan closed the box, then hurled it against the wall. The box exploded into pieces with a shrill clang, and Martin charged forward. He got only three feet before Nolan knocked him aside.

"Martin, no!" Susan cried out.

"Marty!" the children screamed as Nolan grabbed the boy by the throat and pressed the knife against his neck.

"Well, boy, feel brave now, do you?" Nolan asked, laughing as he threw Martin hard against the floor.

"Marty, come here," Ev ordered, grabbing the corner of a bookcase and pulling himself upward until he stood against the wall. "Now!"

Martin scrambled across the room until he was beside his father.

"It's me you're after," Ev said, blinking in hope that the fuzziness would clear from his eyes. "Leave my family alone!"

"You're not the law anymore, Marshal," Nolan retorted. "The only rules now are the ones I make. And mainly they say I can do what I please."

Ev reached out and pulled Martin closer, then placed his left hand on Finley's shoulder. Susan joined them, holding Rachel and Todd tightly.

"No sign of the stage," Buck announced as he reentered the room.

"Then I guess we'd best see about having ourselves something to eat," Nolan said to the Wood boys. "I'm goin' to take myself a walk. Call me when it's ready."

As Nolan retreated, Susan stepped to the table.

"We'd better clean things up," she said, taking a fragment of china from the floor. "Todd, you and Rachel get the broom and sweep up. Fin, you and Martin help me right the table."

The children nodded and hurried to their assignments. Ev fought to steady his legs, but his fingers lacked the power to help. It tore at his heart to watch the others clear the room of its shattered bits of furniture and glass, china and wood.

"I'm so sorry, Susan," Ev said, leaning against her. "Your grandmother's cups. And the music box."

"It doesn't matter," she said, wiping her eyes.

"You loved that music box," Martin said, turning the broken box over in his hands.

"It can be replaced," Susan said. "It all can. The important thing is that we're all fine."

"For how long?" Martin mumbled, looking intently at Ev.

"Enough talk," Ev said, stumbling to the hutch and prying a splinter of glass from its frame. "We've got work to do. Help your mother."

The room grew quiet as Susan and the children started at their tasks. Ev accomplished little. He near fainted twice, and Martin finally helped him to a chair. Once the floor was swept clear of broken china and glass, Susan walked toward the kitchen to get food. She gasped as she reached the door.

"They've been through the rest of the house, too," she told Ev. "Even the mattresses are torn apart."

"I expected as much," he muttered. "Best get one of them to bring you the food. They've been drinkin'. You wouldn't want to surprise them."

"No," she agreed.

Susan called out loudly, and Hazlewood responded. Ben Wood brought in a beef roast and some bread, then warily offered Susan his knife.

"See it's left on the table," Ben said, his dark eyes out of place on a face that couldn't have been more than eighteen years old.

Ev gripped the knife and began slicing the beef. Cutting savagely, he imagined he was plunging the knife into the side of George Nolan, of Hazlewood and the Wood boys.

"You can't do it," Susan said, huddling against him. "You might get one of them, but the others would surely kill you. And the rest of us."

"What are you talkin' about? I'm only carving the meat."

"Are you?" she asked, smiling faintly. "I've seen that look before, lots of times. Know what I'm thinking?"

"No," Ev said, wincing as pain throbbed in his head.

"I was remembering the day we arrived here. Early May, 1878. The twelfth, I think."

"Fourteenth."

"I could hardly believe this was the wonderful place Bill Merritt had described. Three perpetual springs, a forest of trees, a fine house of seven rooms. . . I could see none of it. The water had been fouled by stray cattle. There was a sow running through the dining room. The barn had collapsed. All I could see was a lifetime of work."

"Turned out we had the stable built by summer," Ev said, smiling as he recalled the hours spent with Martin and Finley nailing planks into place and digging a channel diverting the water to a trough for the animals. There'd been pens to build for the pigs, a coop for the chickens, repairs to the roof of the house, not to mention building the ready corral.

"It's strange," Susan said, wiping her eyes. "I never realized what a wonderful home we'd made for ourselves."

"I know," Ev said, sighing. "Sometimes it takes something like this to make you appreciate your good fortune."

"I thought when we left Jacksboro, you'd be safe from. . ."

"Yes," he said. He took her hand. "It's like the war all over again. Everything's torn to pieces. There's no place to hide. And you're all in danger."

Ev slammed his fist against the table and stared angrily out the door.

"If only I'd taken the time to check the posters. If only I'd recognized young Hazlewood in time. If I'd had the Sharps handy when the gambler pulled his pistol. . . . I've handled four men before!"

"We're not dead yet," Martin said, joining them. "Remember, the westbound's got a guard. We can warn 'em, get their help."

"How?" Ev asked, searching his mind for a notion. "And there's no guarantee of anything."

Martin nodded, and Susan clutched Ev's hand.

"All I've thought of for the last year was that note signed to buy this place," Ev said, intertwining his fingers with Susan's. "Another year of stages, a few horses sold, and our cattle driven to market would pay the balance. And now?"

Nolan sauntered into the room again, and Ev's other thoughts vanished. He saw only the outlaw's grimy face, the thinning black hair and the dark, hate-filled eyes.

The children shrank back from Nolan's glance, even Martin. Terror again raced through little Todd and Finley. Rachel hid behind her mother.

"Don't take to your Uncle George, eh?" Nolan jeered as Finley clutched his father's arm.

"I'm glad my uncles are dead," Martin said, the words cutting the air like the knife in his father's hand. "They fell in the war. Better that than turned into a lyin' killer like you!"

"Best teach this boy some respect, Marshal!" Nolan snarled, turning suddenly and shoving Martin across the room. "You're not so young, cub, that I wouldn't kill you."

"Go ahead!" Martin shouted, tears appearing in his eyes. "You probably will anyway."

"Martin!" Susan screamed.

But it was the blazing eyes of his father that attracted Martin's attention. Ev rapped the table, and Martin reluctantly retreated.

"See you've got our supper ready," Nolan said, helping himself to a slice of bread. "I believe it's time we cleared you on out of here, Marshal."

"Nolan then called to Hazlewood, and Rip walked in cradling a long-barreled Winchester in his arms.

"Best come along with me," Hazlewood said to the family, pointing toward the door.

"We'll call you when we're through," Nolan said, grinning.

"Where. . ."

"The storeroom," Hazlewood said, hesitating momentarily. "The others are already in there. You have to understand. . ."

"He has to understand nothin'!" Nolan shouted. "Get him out of here, Rip!"

Hazlewood again pointed toward the door, and Susan helped Ev to his feet. With Martin's help, Ev struggled through the door and around to the storeroom. Ben Wood swung open the door, and Ev led the way inside. He saw in the faint light that the barrels and boxes had been ransacked. Art Hyland lay in the far corner, nursing a lump on the side of his face. The gambler lay in a heap beside the door.

"You all right, Marty?" Hazlewood asked as the children trickled through the door.

"Don't talk to me," Martin replied bitterly. "You lied! You let them hurt my father!"

"I did what I had to," Hazlewood said, searching for sympathy from Ev. "I always do."

"You lie, you rob, and you kill," Susan said, drawing the children to her side. "Leave us alone."

Ben laughed, then swung the door of the storeroom shut. Hazlewood remained outside a moment, then headed on back to the house. Ev blinked as the darkness settled in all around them.

"They're after the westbound," Art said.

"I know," Ev told the driver. "How's the gambler?"

"Bleedin's stopped. Shot went clean through. He'll be all right. Thought it best he slept."

"It is," Susan said.

"They made a pretty big mess of the house," Ev explained. "They've got the guns."

"Went through your pockets, too," Art said. "Mine as well. That's how I picked up this little souvenir."

Art pointed to his head as Ev felt his empty pockets. The crisp bills Hazlewood had exchanged for the mustang were gone. So was the watch. The only other money in the house was concealed beneath the floorboards of the bedroom. Perhaps Nolan hadn't located it. And even if he had, there wasn't more than a few dollars.

Ev sank onto the dusty floor of the storeroom. Susan rested her head on his shoulder again, and Rachel climbed up one knee.

"How's my little girl?" Ev asked as cheerfully as he could manage.

Rachel said nothing, just rocked back and forth. Finley squeezed in between Susan and a barrel of flour. Todd crawled over, and Ev wrapped an arm around the boy's sweat-streaked shoulders. Martin sat on the opposite side of Todd, breathing heavily as if a great weight rested on his young chest.

It was the perfect prison, that storeroom. The cracks between the plank sides of the building allowed little more than a glimpse of the world outside, and the darkness added to the terror. Ev felt the trembling shoulders of the children, heard their labored breathing. Todd whimpered, clawing Ev's arm with small, desperate fingers.

"Pa?" Todd asked between sobs.

"I'm here," Ev said, stroking the boy's soft hair. "Don't worry, son."

"We're all goin' to die," Finley said, shuddering.

"No, we're goin' to get out of this," Ev said.

"How?" Martin asked.

"We'll find a way," Ev told them all. "Don't fret. There've been tough times for the Raymonds before."

"Tough as this?" Fin asked.

Ev didn't, couldn't answer. He held Rachel tightly and searched for a reply. His ears fought to ignore the sobs, did their best not to hear the gambler's moaning or Art's mumbled curses. Overhead sacks of onions and turnips mixed pungently with the damp, sand floor to fill the storeroom with an overpowering odor, a smell of rot and decay. . . of death.

Ev did his best to erase those images from his mind, to think of better, happier times. But always the vision of George Nolan's wicked, hateful eyes returned. In that violent, unshaven face, all the worst traits of man seemed to combine. In the sinister eyes and razor-sharp tongue Ev read his death, foresaw all that a man most fears for himself and his family.

Oh, Lord, help me find a solution, Ev prayed. He imagined the westbound breaking a wheel or busting an axle. Anything to give them a little more time. But in the end, he knew it would be up to only one man. . . Ev Raymond.

He touched Todd's cold, damp shoulder, then squeezed Rachel's tiny wrists. Susan's head stirred slightly on his shoulder, and Ev muffled a sob. Finally he closed his eyes and let the darkness swallow his troubles.

CHAPTER 5

AS the dizziness and pain eased, Ev began studying the situation. Through the cracks in the planking, he was able to examine the front corner of the house and the dusty ground lying between it and the stable. To anyone not familiar with the little station at Antelope Springs, the view wouldn't have provided many clues to what was happening. But to Ev, each blade of grass was familiar. An enlarged shadow behind the woodpile told him an outlaw lay hidden there. The glint of steel flashing in the afternoon sunlight hinted another was atop the roof of the stable.

The young ones'll be there, Ev told himself. Nolan would be in the house, keeping out of view. His face was well known among the stage drivers. Hazlewood would likely be in plain sight, his easy manners concealing the peril awaiting the westbound.

"The stage's late," Martin said, sitting beside his father and trying to catch a glimpse of the outlaws. "Another one rode in a while back."

"Another one?" Ev asked in alarm. "Who?"

"Lou Stacy," Art said, spitting. "Should've known someone from the line was in on it. How else'd they know which route to hit?"

"Lou Stacy," Ev mumbled, picturing in his mind Stacy's fifty-year-old face, the tired eyes and wrinkled forehead. Stacy'd fought Comanches and renegade soldiers for twenty years. Recently he'd taken to drinking heavily, and the line had dropped him as a driver. Last Ev heard, Stacy was tending the counter of a dry goods store in Albany. The store stood alongside the freight office.

"It makes good sense, when you think on it," Art said, spitting again. "Takin' two coaches at one time. Only thing is, there was mighty little profit in hittin' our outfit. Don't suppose we had fifty dollars amongst us."

"It was a good way of takin' the station, though," Ev said, recalling how Buck was hidden inside the coach. Nobody'd suspect a youngster like that of being in with the Nolan gang. Buck had disarmed Art, tended to the gambler. And with the job of changing teams, Ev had had little time to watch for riders.

"Know what's on the westbound?" Art asked.

"They don't pass the figures along," Ev explained. "But bein' the end of the month, could be ranch payrolls aboard."

"I heard it was five, ten thousand," Art said. "That means there'll be a guard. Young Shipley's the driver. There's two good men. They can make a fight of it."

"Provided Nolan hasn't got a man on that coach, too," Ev said, gazing through the cracks again. "I wouldn't be surprised. Not one bit."

"You figure they'll leave us locked up in here till they're through, Pa?" Martin asked.

"No," Ev told the boy. "First sign of the stage, they'll want us out there. Tom Shipley's young, but he'd know somethin' was up if we were gone."

"Then we can warn 'em," Fin said, slapping his knee. "It'll be like the time you captured the Jimersons, Pa."

"Only two of them," Ev said, "and I was the one with the gun. First sign of a warnin', Nolan'd shoot. Maybe me. Maybe your ma. No, we'll get no chance to warm 'em, son."

"Your pa's right," Art said. "Nolan's been at this game a long time. Our best chance is to hope the stage's late. Then maybe they'll get careless, give us a chance to slip away."

"Won't be easy," Ev said, tapping the heavy cedar planks

of the storeroom. "I built this place to last. We might dig our way out somewhere else, but this ground's solid rock."

"If only we had a pistol," Art grumbled.

"We do," a feeble voice declared.

All eyes turned toward the gambler. The wounded man groaned as he sat up.

"You've got a gun?" Art asked. "Where?"

"My boot," the gambler said, lifting his left foot. Martin and Finley helped the stranger remove the boot. Hidden in the heel was a tiny two-shot Colt Derringer.

"Not much of an arsenal," Ev admitted.

"Might get us past one man. Then we'd have his gun, too," the gambler said. "Way I see it, they're bound to send somebody out to bring us food."

"I wouldn't count on that," Ev said.

"Well, to see we're still here, at least," the gambler went on. "We take him by surprise. Then we close in on the house, get the rifles. Now we've got a better'n even chance."

"Of gettin' shot to pieces," Ev said. "Maybe you don't know it, but Nolan's got a man on the stable roof, another past the woodpile. Anything happens, they'd have a clear field of fire. We'd be pinned down in here.

"We've got to try," Martin said. "I run fast. I could try for the one behind the woodpile. Hit him with a board, maybe."

"If it was the three of us," Ev said to Art and the gambler, "I'd be with you. But I've got a wife and four kids in here. Whatever we do, they'll share the risk."

"You don't know Nolan," the gambler said, motioning for the boys to replace the boot. "He'll kill us either way. He's not one to leave witnesses."

Ev glanced around him at the fearful eyes of Susan and the children. Only Rachel seemed not to understand.

"I'm for tryin'," Art said.

"Me, too," the gambler declared.

"I'm for studyin' things a bit more," Ev said. "We're tired. I've got a pumpkin for a skull, and the gambler there's shot through. Tonight, when it's dark'd be best. Mornin' even better."

"Ev, stage'll likely be here 'fore that," Art reminded him.

"Maybe. On the other hand, they had a hard rain off to the east night before last. Could be the trail's bogged. Ford might be swollen."

"Pray it's so," Art said, restlessly gazing out a small hole in the wall.

Time appeared to stand still in the storeroom. It was impossible to tell what hour it really was. Ev could normally read the sky, tell by the color and position of the sun. But inside, with clouds overhead, it was hard to tell if it was near sunset. Twice the growing darkness turned out to be a heavy cloud blocking the sun.

"Pa, you hear that?" little Todd asked suddenly.

"What?" Ev asked, growing alert. "Did you hear wheels? Is the stage here?"

"No," Todd said, creeping over closer. "It's the chickens. I didn't get to feed 'em. They'll be hungry."

"I'm hungry myself," Martin said. "And thirsty."

Ev swallowed hard. Truth was, they were all in need of food and water. He angrily thought about the cool liquid bubbling out of the springs, the tender roast beef he'd sliced for Nolan's thieves.

"Hey!" Ev shouted toward the woodpile. "Hey!"

"Quit your hollerin', Marshal," Ben Wood yelled back. "I've got no time for it."

Ev tried again, stopping only when he saw the long barrel of a Winchester train itself on the storeroom.

"Another word," shouted Ben, "and I'll answer you with this."

The gun wobbled, and Ev surrendered. He located a tin of peaches and managed to poke holes in its top with a nail. Each of the children sipped a bit of juice. That

soothed the worst of their thirst, and a second can was
passed among the adults. With some difficulty, Art pried
open the lid, and half a peach was enjoyed by each of the
captives.

"I've eaten better," Susan said, laughing as she dropped
a peach pit into the empty tin. "I suppose this is one time
even Finley'd eat his greens."

The children laughed, too, and Finley seemed to
brighten.

"If only we had a little music," Susan said, sighing.

"That man busted your box!" Martin said, jumping to
his feet and running to the door of the storeroom. He
banged against the heavy planking and yelled. No one
appeared to hear, and Ev finally tugged the boy away.

"Maybe we can hum a tune," Susan suggested.

"Pa, we've got to do something," Martin declared. "We
can't just sit here and wait for them to. . ."

"That's enough of that," Ev said, sitting the boy down
on the floor. "Sometimes patience is your strongest
weapon. You have to await your opportunities."

"I'm not sure I can," Martin said, gripping his father's
arm tightly. "I just don't know. . ."

"Did I ever tell you children about the time your
grandfather and I hid out from Comanche Indians?" Ev
asked.

"Tell us," Susan said, wrapping one arm around Rachel
and the other around Todd. Ev pulled Finley over, and
all six of them formed a half-circle opposite Art Hyland
and the gambler.

"I suppose I was no older than Fin, here," Ev began,
waving his hand through Finley's hair and squeezing the
boy's neck. "It was a few years after Pa returned from the
Mexican War. Ma and my brother Barrett were off visiting Grandma Sanders—sure I haven't told you this before?"

The children's heads shook back and forth in spite of

the fact that Ev had shared the tale two dozen times.

"Well, anyway," Ev continued, "those Comanches never did take to us buildin' a cabin on land they considered was theirs. Once or twice a year they'd swoop down on us like red-tailed hawks, burnin' barns and cabins, killin' any men they found in the open, carryin' off women and children to be their slaves."

Ev felt Fin shudder, and Rachel gasped. Art nodded, and even the gambler cracked a smile.

"Well, I guess you know Pa and I were none too happy to see a dozen bare-chested Indians ridin' toward us, their faces painted half black, half white. Comanche death face, Pa told me. They were out for glory or death. Didn't matter much to them. And we were out in the cornfields, barefooted, with not so much as a good skinnin' knife between us."

"What happened then?" Todd asked.

"Well, Todd, the corn was already nigh as high as I was," Ev told the boy. "Pa got on his knees, and we just stood there, still as statues. The Comanches rode through the field, here and there, babblin' away in words I couldn't understand. Then we saw smoke. They'd set our cabin afire. Everything we owned was burnin' up. And we couldn't do a thing besides sit there and pretend we were frozen."

"With the Indians all around you?" Todd asked.

"Close enough you could smell what they'd eaten for breakfast," Ev explained. "So close you'd swear they had to know you were there. They did a fair bit of lookin' for us, but finally they gave up."

"And you escaped," Fin said.

"Sure did," Ev declared, smiling at Susan through the dim light.

"Lucky he did," Martin said, "else we wouldn't be here now."

"See, little ones," Ev said, lightly touching first Rachel,

then Todd and Finley and Martin on the forehead. "Didn't seem a chance in a hundred of gettin' through that alive, but we did. And we'll survive this, too."

"How?" Martin asked.

"We'll find out quick enough," the gambler said, pointing toward the door. Two pairs of footsteps approached, one somewhat heavy, the other lighter. The gambler drew out the Derringer, but Ev grabbed it away.

"They'll expect somethin' now," Ev said, hiding the small pistol in a flour barrel. "Later, when we're rested, and they're growin' edgy. Once I read the lay of the land. Then we'll make our move."

"Remember the children," Susan pleaded.

Art nodded, and the gambler surrendered. Without the pistol, there wasn't a whole lot could be done anyway.

"I'll hold you to your words, stationmaster," the gambler said, staring at the door. "Tonight, or at worst, tomorrow morning."

Ev nodded, then stood up and gathered Susan and the children into the back corner of the room.

"Ev?" she asked.

Then a key turned in the lock, and the heavy door swung open.

CHAPTER 6

THE bright light that flooded the storeroom blinded Ev. He covered his eyes and tried to identify the shadowy figures in the doorway. When his eyes adjusted to the light, he discovered Rip Hazlewood holding a Winchester and smiling out a greeting.

"Say, Marty, you back there?" Hazlewood asked. "Ever know the westbound stage to be this late before?"

Martin glanced at his father, but Hazlewood stepped inside and pushed Ev aside.

"Well, boy?" Hazlewood demanded.

"All the time," Martin said. " 'Course, I don't know what time it is now. I can remember the westbound comin' in two, three days behind schedule.

"He's lyin'," Nolan said, joining Hazlewood inside the storeroom. "It'll be on in soon enough."

"Then we ought to get them outside, don't you think, Uncle George?" Hazlewood said, poking the barrel of the rifle into Ev's ribs. "Driver's bound to grow suspicious if he sees the place deserted."

"Thought you said there'd be plenty of time to bring 'em out once Lou spots the stage," Nolan said. "Why change the plan? Not goin' soft on me, are you, Rip?"

"I can be hard as there's need," Hazlewood said, the smile vanishing from his face. "You know that, Uncle George. You're not needin' a sample of my work at this point, I hope."

Hazlewood pointed the rifle at the gambler and laughed.

"Well, I don't suppose it'd hurt to let 'em out for a

time," Nolan conceded. "You tell Ben to take the lady to the kitchen. She can start our dinner. You watch the marshal personally. He and the boys can tend the stock. The rest stay here."

"You can't leave Rachel by herself," Susan objected. "She can help me in the kitchen."

"Maybe you want the gambler in there, too," Nolan jeered.

"Ben can watch two women," Hazlewood said. "Like as not, they'll all watch their step if he's got an eye on that little girl."

"Could be," Nolan grumbled. "But the driver and the gambler stay put. Once the food's ready, you have Ben send the woman and her kid back in here, too. We may need Marshal Raymond here outside for show, but not the others."

Hazlewood nodded, then shouted for Ben to come over. Ev gave Susan's hand a gentle squeeze, then patted Rachel lightly on her head. They left then, shepherded along by Ben Wood.

"Now, I guess it's time we got along to our work, Marshal," Hazlewood said, pointing toward the storeroom door.

Ev nodded, then motioned for the boys to follow. Martin followed Hazlewood, but Ev had to lead Finley and Todd along by the hand. Once outside, though, the boys seemed more at ease.

"Can I feed the chickens now?" Todd asked, pointing to the birds in the coop. "They're probably pretty hungry."

"That all right?" Ev asked Hazlewood.

"Go ahead," the gunman said. "Tend to what you usually do. Just keep in mind Ben's with your ma, boys. And Buck's on the roof."

"You hear him?" Ev asked, his eyes growing deadly serious. "Do just like you always do. Keep in sight, too. No wanderin', not today."

"Yes, sir," Finley said, starting toward the stable.

"Sure, Pa," Todd added as he took the feed bag and headed for the coop.

Ev himself waved to Martin, then glanced around. The horses were still hitched to the eastbound coach. The animals could be fed and watered easy enough, then put in stalls. The relief team he'd planned to use for the eastbound pranced nervously in the ready corral. They'd do for the westbound. But the stage couldn't be left standing outside the stable.

"What do I do with the coach?" Ev asked Hazlewood. "It's as out of place as a brass band."

"Can you stow it in the stable?"

"Not a prayer," Ev explained. "It's too high and too wide for the doors."

Hazlewood looked around for some hint of a solution. Finding none, he called for Nolan.

"Get Lou to drive it out away, west," Nolan ordered. "He can unhitch the horses and bring 'em back. Leave the coach in a gully."

"My pleasure," Stacy said, waving Ev away from the harness. "Always wanted to wreck a stage."

"Someone's bound to notice an overturned coach," Ev pointed out.

"And who'd that be?" Nolan asked, turning his rifle toward Ev. "Got lots of neighbors, do you? Who'd they tell? Why, they'd ride over and have a talk with the stationmaster, wouldn't they? Good thing we're here, isn't it?"

Nolan laughed heartily, and Stacy joined in. Then the former driver mounted the stage and whipped the horses into motion. As the coach vanished in a cloud of choking dust, Ev helped Martin fill the water troughs. The horses immediately lapped at the water, and Ev himself poured two cupfuls down his throat.

"Can we take some water to Art and the gambler?" Martin asked Hazlewood. "They haven't had any since mornin'."

"When you finish," Hazlewood said. "Wouldn't want to bother Uncle George for the key just now."

Martin nodded, then continued pouring buckets of water into the corral troughs.

"How come you got yourself mixed up with them?" Marty asked, pointing first at Buck Wood, then swinging his long index finger toward the house where Nolan lay stretched out on the porch.

"When my folks died, Uncle George looked after me," Hazlewood said. "He took in Ben and Buck, too."

"Looked after you?" Ev mocked. "That what you call it? He'll see you all hung more likely."

"What would you know about it?" Hazlewood shouted. "You marshals! You hide behind your lawbooks and judges. When it comes down to it, we're not all that different. We steal because we need the money. Yankee taxes took our farm."

"I lost everything in the war, too," Ev said. "Most did. But you don't start preyin' on everybody else."

"Isn't that what you did? Tell me the difference, Marshal. You hunted us like a man'd hunt a wolf. And there were those who paid you to kill."

"You broke the law," Martin said.

"Yankee laws, made by Yankees."

"I recall somethin' about 'Thou shalt not kill,' " Ev said, leading Martin away. "You can always find a reason for breakin' laws if you try hard enough. Truth is you'd rather steal than earn money the hard way, sweatin' away buildin' a place, tendin' stock and plantin' fields."

"Fool's labor," Hazlewood growled, glancing at his cousin Buck.

If Hazlewood had been paying closer attention to Martin, the horses might never have escaped. Actually, the stagecoach team remained at the trough. But the mustangs, all seven of them, took to the hills the second Martin swung open the gate and slapped his knee.

"Yah! Yah!" Marty hollered as the horses raced away.

"What the. . ." Nolan cried out, jumping to his feet.

"The horses!" Buck yelled. "They're gettin' away!"

The mustangs, joined by the three saddle mounts ridden in by Nolan's men, turned a wild circle past the hill. Nolan stormed over, and Ev ran to intercept the outlaw. Martin was still yelling at the horses when Nolan arrived. Ev stared in horror as Nolan drove the butt of his rifle into Marty's chest, then kicked the stunned boy in the side.

"Leave him be!" Ev yelled, his vision suddenly blurring as he stumbled toward his son.

"It's you put him up to it, no doubt," Nolan snarled. "I ought to shoot him dead. Right here and now."

"No!" Hazlewood pleaded. "The shot."

"There's other ways," Nolan said, pulling a Bowie knife from his belt. "Could carve a few notches in his hide. Boy of mine did such a thing, he'd bleed for a month."

"Pa!" Martin cried, terror filling his eyes.

"Look," Ev said, pointing to the animals. Most of the horses congregated near the water hole.

"Rip, you take that boy and round 'em up," Nolan said, spitting on the ground beside Martin's head. "Lock the marshal and the others in the storeroom first. That boy so much as flinches, you put a ball through his head. Understand?"

"I understand," Hazlewood said, turning to Martin. "You believe I'll do it, too, Marty. Look to your pa. He knows I will."

"Do as you're told, Marty," Ev pleaded.

Martin started to say something, but Ev stared the words away.

"Don't you see he could've killed you?" Ev asked. "And what did it accomplish? Nothing."

"You got a good head on those shoulders, Marshal," Nolan said, scratching his head. "Next one steps out of line, though, there'll be a price paid."

Nolan then reached over and took Finley's arm. The Bowie knife flashed, tearing a great slice through the front of Finley's overalls and leaving a shallow cut two or three inches across on the boy's chest.

"I'll see you dead if. . ." Ev began.

"Next time I'll cut deeper," Nolan said, throwing Finley against his father. "Maybe I'll choose to work on the little one," he added, pointing to Todd. "Maybe the missus. Can't tell. Don't do anything that might lead you to find out. Hear me?"

"I hear you," Ev said. "Did you hear me?"

"Still hasn't lost his bluster, no sir," Nolan told young Buck. "'Course it's pure amazin' how quick a Bowie knife can cut that bluster out of a man."

Finley tried to rush at Nolan, but Ev pinned the boy's arms.

"That's enough," Ev said, gripping the twelve-year-old tightly. "This isn't the time, son."

But the fire in Finley's eyes ignored the words.

"Get 'em locked up again," Nolan commanded.

"But what if the stage. . ."

"Lock 'em up!" Nolan yelled, kicking a stone onto the porch. "Lock 'em up before I turn this knife on you!"

Hazlewood swung his rifle at Todd, and Ev motioned for the boy to drop his feedbag and return to the storeroom. Ev then dragged a rebellious Finley along.

"You shouldn't have let the horses go, Marty," Hazlewood said as he used his uncle's key to unlock the door. Then, as Ev and the younger boys stepped inside, Hazlewood pressed his rifle barrel against Marty's neck.

"Go ahead," Martin said. "Shoot me."

"I will if it comes to that," Hazlewood said. "I don't want to bring harm to any of you, though. Tell them, Marshal. Explain I'm just doin' what I'm told."

"You had lots of choices," Ev said, glaring at Hazlewood, "You didn't have to stay. You might've warned us."

"They're my kin, for better or not," Hazlewood replied, his eyes turning suddenly cold.

"I wouldn't brag on it," Marty said.

"Was only statin' a fact," Hazlewood declared as he slammed the door shut and clamped the lock. "Now come along. We've got horses to round up."

Once George Nolan cooled off a bit, he allowed Ev to help bring in the horses. It proved a busy time, what with Lou Stacy returning with the coachless team. Finally the last of the animals were safely put in a stall or led to the corral.

"Lot of wasted effort," the gambler grumbled when Hazlewood returned Ev and Martin to their storeroom prison.

"Not all," Martin said, grinning. "Good thing they can't count, Pa. Otherwise they'd notice we came up one short."

"Star's still gone," Todd announced, referring to the mustang with the splash of white across his nose. "Wonder if he'll go wild again."

"Horse like that's one to notice," Art said, sipping a cup of water Ev had managed to smuggle into the storeroom. "Could be help will come."

"Possible," Ev said, trying to lift their hopes. Deep down he knew only the Merritts would likely see the horse or the stage, either one, and Bill Merritt and his two oldest boys wouldn't stand much of a chance against Nolan's bunch.

Ev struggled with a terrible sense of futility as they day dragged on. The stage failed to appear, and Nolan's curses drifted across from the house, frightening Todd and stirring Martin to shout occasional replies.

"Your mother's still in the house," Ev reminded Martin.

For a time the boy would walk off to one corner and huddle against a barrel of flour. But later he would storm to the door and gaze with hateful eyes at the outlaws.

Ev was greatly relieved when Susan finally returned.

"We're to join them for dinner," she said, motioning to Art and the wounded gambler as well.

"Wonder what brought this on?" Ev asked, lifting little Rachel onto his weary shoulders and wrapping an arm around Todd.

"Oh, Uncle George's got a real kind heart," Ben said, covering them with his rifle. "Now let's walk nice and easy on over to the house. Wouldn't want to disturb a good meal by shootin' anybody."

Once they gathered around the table, Ev discovered the purpose of George Nolan's invitation. Nolan spent a full hour relating a series of daring holdups and grand adventures. It was more entertaining than listening to Harlan Daley's tales from the war. Todd and Finley listened eagerly. Ev frowned at the brightness in their eyes.

How quickly boys can forget, Ev thought. Well, maybe that was best. He wondered if they might be able to forget this day equally fast. He hoped so.

Susan said nothing through the first three stories. But when Nolan described a bank robbery in Gainesville, she managed to knock a pot of scalding coffee onto the table. Steaming liquid splattered Nolan's hands, and he rose howling from his chair.

"I'm so sorry," Susan cried, righting the pot and doing her best to soak up the coffee with her table napkin. Ev fought a smile from his face. Ordinarily she'd no more stain a good napkin with coffee than shoot herself. Likely she assumed the linens would go the way of her china.

"I'll take that to've been an accident," Nolan said after spreading lard on his burned hands. "But if there's another one, some little girl might break an arm."

Susan glanced at Rachel and turned pale.

"Now, as I was sayin'," Nolan continued.

"Why not tell them the truth for once," Ev said, standing up. "I know all about Gainesville. You were in town early on a Sunday morning. You took the banker's wife and daughter captive, then forced him to open the vault. No sooner had you got the cash than you shot all three of them, banker, wife, and daughter. How old was the girl, Nolan, fourteen?"

"Old enough," Stacy said, grinning.

"Old as she ever got to be," Buck added.

"The wife died, too," Ev said, speaking especially to his sons. "Then there was the widow Harper walkin' to church with her youngest, little Billy. Husband and four older boys all fell with Terry's rangers."

"They surprised us," Hazlewood said, nervously pushing himself back from the table. "We didn't know it was a woman and a boy. All we heard was a shout. Then there they were."

"You killed the woman right away, but the boy. . . how many shots did you put in him, Nolan? Five? Six? How many times can you kill a boy of ten?"

"That's younger'n me," Finley said, shivering.

"Is all that true?" Martin asked Hazlewood. "The women, too?"

"We do what we have to do," Hazlewood said, staring bitterly at his uncle. "When you set out to rob a place, you know you may have to kill anyone who gets in the way."

"Like us?" Martin asked. "Me and my folks?"

"There'll be no need of that," Nolan said as he tore the seal off a bottle of Canadian whiskey looted from the storeroom. "Not as long as you cooperate. And you'll do just that, won't you, Marshal? Oh, I'm sorry. It's stationmaster now, isn't it?"

"That's right," Ev said, his face glowing scarlet. "But you boys sure do fire the urge to return to my former line of work."

"That wouldn't be healthy," Nolan said, grinning. "We never leave a marshal behind to track us, do we, boys?"

"Way I hear it," the gambler said, "you never leave anyone. Not alive, that is."

"Oh, we do now and again," Nolan told them. "Just depends on the odds. We make a big haul with that westbound tomorrow, we'll be able to get ourselves away from Texas."

"Tomorrow?" Ev asked.

"Seems late for it to get here today," Nolan said. "Lou says the driver's bound to put up for the night along the way. Can't cross the Brazos after sundown."

"You mean to lock us up all night, with no food or water?" Susan asked.

"You can fill yourself a bucket of water. I'll even let you take some bread."

"What about bedclothes?" she asked. "Blankets?"

"I'm afraid we've been a little to playful with those things," Buck remarked, breaking into a wide grin. "Guess you'll have to make do with what you've got."

Ev frowned as Buck hovered over Susan's shoulder and whispered something in her ear.

"I'd suggest you back away!" Ev shouted.

"Or what?" Buck asked, turning toward Ev and pulling a pistol quick as a cat.

"She might find herself another pot of coffee," Stacy joked.

The others chuckled, and Buck returned his gun to its holster.

"Later, Marshal," Buck spoke through clenched teeth. "After we've tended to the stage, we'll tend to you."

"Yeah, we'll be doin' that," Nolan agreed. "Sure as the sun comes up, we'll be doin' that."

CHAPTER 7

HAZLEWOOD and young Ben Wood escorted Ev, Art Hyland, the gambler, and the boys back to the storeroom. The sun was dipping below the horizon, and there was a cold, damp smell inside the storeroom. Art kept the boys occupied with stories of the wild days of the frontier. Ev sat beside the padlocked door and waited for Susan to arrive.

"She'll be on along, Ev," Art said more than once. "They won't be harmin' her with little Rachel there."

"They won't do anything yet," the gambler agreed. "Not so long as they need you to welcome that stage. But afterward. . ."

"I know," Ev said somberly.

"Then you know tomorrow morning's our best chance to break up this little party of theirs," the gambler said.

Ev nodded, but as the gambler and Art debated plans, Ev heard nothing. His thoughts were a hundred yards away in the kitchen, washing tin plates and putting away uneaten scraps of food.

It was pitch dark when Susan finally returned. The door swung open, allowing a breath of cool evening air to seep into the stifling room. Susan and little Rachel stepped inside, and the door slammed shut. The air was as bad as ever, and the water bucket hadn't been refilled. Ev sighed and wrapped an arm around Rachel. He then embraced Susan with the other.

"They didn't mistreat you?" he asked.

"No," she said, stooping over to greet each of the boys in turn. "Young Rip Hazlewood stood watch. He isn't like his uncle, Ev. Given half a chance, I think he'd let us go."

"Don't count on that, ma'am," the gambler objected. "He hides it better than most, but deep down he's a killer. I'd rather face a cougar in the open than a snake in the tall grass."

"Ben doesn't seem so bad, either," Martin said. "It's Buck and Nolan we've got to worry about."

"Don't rule out Lou Stacy," Art added. "He's a great one for shootin' at a man's back. We always did lose money when he kept his own accounts."

"I heard that," Ev said, "but Stacy's no gunman. I'd say Nolan's enough of a worry for all of us. He's not one to avoid gunplay, and he's cold as a January norther about killin'."

"So Nolan's the one we'd like to take out first," the gambler said, chewing on a blade of grass. "Only he's not likely to be the one waking us in the morning. More likely it'll be Hazlewood, or one of the young ones."

"Not Buck," Ev said, pointing at the ceiling. "Nolan'll want him watchin' the road."

"Then it could be Stacy," Art said. "More likely Hazlewood and Ben. We ought to be able to surprise those two."

"And then what?" Ev asked. "Nolan's unlikely to just ride off, not where ten thousand dollars is involved."

"There'll be three left," the gambler noted. "We'll have guns, but we'll have to move fast, take the rest before they have a chance to see what's happening."

"And where will the children be all this time?" Susan asked, standing up angrily. "I'll tell you. They'll be in here dodging gunfire. One stray shot, and somebody could easily get killed. What about you yourselves? You'll be in the open. You couldn't hit Buck Wood if you tried. As for Nolan, he'd have his choice of targets."

"She's right," Ev admitted. "Still, I don't see we've got much choice. The stage isn't goin' to be too much later."

"No," Art agreed. "It's tomorrow or never. They could

come in here and search the place anytime. They'd find the pistol, and we'd be finished."

"So, tell us the rest of it," Ev said, turning to the gambler's shadowy face. "What happens once we disarm Hazlewood and Stacy, or whoever they may be?"

"First, we stay as quiet as we can," the gambler explained. "Next, we split up. One of us best cover the man on the roof. Someone else can clear out the house. Where's the third man?"

"Back of the woodpile," Ev said.

"That's near the barn?"

"Stable," Ev grumbled. "So, who goes where?"

"I can't see Art climbin' a roof," Martin said, creeping over.

"I'll try the house," Art said, his voice slightly shaky.

"You'd best cover the first pair," Ev told the gambler. "You don't look up to anything more."

"No," the gambler agreed. "But that leaves two for you, the one at the woodpile and the man on the roof."

"I can. . ." Martin offered.

"No," Ev declared, patting Martin's shoulder. "There's no way to get to the roof without passin' young Ben at the woodpile. I'll take Ben, then see what can be done about Buck up there on the roof. It's goin' to be tricky. You can see everything from there."

"It all sounds so foolhardy," Susan announced. "You'll only get yourselves killed. Are we that desperate?"

Ev glanced at the faint faces of the others. Their eyes seemed hauntingly distant. Only the gambler appeared confident, decided. Art Hyland was lost. No hint of hope remained in the driver's weary glance. Terror crept across the faces of the children. Even Marty, taking the first awkward steps toward manhood, was shaking. But in spite of himself, Ev couldn't see a splinter of a chance that the gambler's plan would succeed.

"What do you expect the children and me to do while

you're trying to get yourself shot?" Susan asked, turning Ev's face back toward her own.

"You have to find a way of slippin' out," Ev whispered, clutching her hand. "Maybe you can get out past the water hole, hide out. Later you might get to the Merritt place."

"Wouldn't it be easier just to return to the house?" she asked.

He avoided her probing eyes. No, they wouldn't be willing to return to the house, those eyes said. Because George Nolan will still be in that house, shooting at the rest of them. But how could Susan get Todd and Rachel far? Even with Finley and Marty to help, could they really escape?

"We've got fair hope for success ma'am," the gambler said, taking the pistol from its hiding place in the flour barrel. "And even if we fail, we'll fare no worse than we would otherwise. This leaves us a chance."

"We have to try," Ev said, pulling Susan closer.

"I've seen Nolan's eyes, too," she said. "But there's help coming. Surely the westbound stage will be here tomorrow. You said yourself it'll have a guard."

"Susan. . ."

"Ev Raymond, you're not a lawman anymore. There's no star on your shirt," she told him. "You don't owe anyone anything. No one's paying you to fight outlaws now!"

I don't owe anyone anything? Ev asked himself. I owe my family don't I? I owe the westbound a fighting chance. But he kept his thoughts to himself.

"Ev?" she asked, huddling against him.

"It's time we got our rest," he said, leading her to the far side of the little room. "Tomorrow promises to be a long day."

She nodded her agreement, then began spacing the children along the wall. Art sprawled out on the opposite wall, and the gambler resumed his place beside the door.

"I wish we had Ma's music box," Martin grumbled as he

pulled off his boots. "I remember how it used to chase off the fright of summer storms."

"Or howlin' wolves," Finley added, abandoning his assigned place between Todd and Rachel. "A story might help."

"Your pa's tired, boys," Susan told them. "Don't forget he's had a hard rap on the head. Leave him to his sleep."

"Sure, Ma," Fin said, slipping out of his overalls and lying down on the hard ground beside Martin.

Susan helped little Rachel out of her dress, then covered the sleepy child with a sheet of canvas taken from the storage shelf.

"Can I sleep here?" Todd asked, indicating the sliver of ground between Ev and Susan.

"Scared?" Ev asked, resting his hands on the boy's sweaty shoulders.

"Some," Todd admitted.

"Don't you think you'll be all right over there by Rachel? Your sister's probably a little frightened, too."

"I'll guard her," Todd said, giving Ev a rare hug before departing.

Once the children appeared settled, Ev lay back and stared at the darkness overhead. The stars were up there, but the roof of the storeroom hid them from view. A stillness settled in around them, disturbed only by crickets chirping down at the water hole and Art snoring across the room. The children stirred, trying to find a comfortable sleeping posture. Finley couldn't curl up as he normally did for lack of space, and Marty had to bend his legs to avoid the gambler's feet.

Susan rested her head on Ev's chest. It felt good having her close. Ordinarily Susan fell into a sound sleep straight away, but Ev heard her labored breathing, felt her trembling fingers intertwine with his own.

"I've tried never to hate anyone," she whispered, "but that Nolan! I can't help myself, Ev. I wish he were dead."

"He wouldn't be missed by me," he replied, kissing her forehead.

"I don't see how you can be so calm."

"Is that what I am?" he asked, showing her his trembling hand. "I try not to let the little ones see."

"What're we going to do?"

"I don't know," he confessed. "What we can. Maybe they'll make a mistake. It's happened before."

"I've looked into Nolan's eyes. He's the devil. He'll kill you, Ev."

"Not till the stage arrives," Ev whispered, kissing her a second time. "Till then he needs me."

"And afterward?"

"Nobody knows the future, Susan. I've seen things turn before, though. Maybe tomorrow mornin' the gambler's plan will work."

"You don't believe that."

"It doesn't matter," Ev muttered, holding her tightly. "I told you before. We have to try."

Ev slipped into a light sleep then, leaving his worries behind. But it wasn't that easy to escape. A face appeared, cloudlike, distorted, snarling with what seemed to be wolf's teeth. Eyes bore in like angry balls of fire.

"I told you, Marshal," a terrifying voice spoke, "we'd tend to you."

A hand appeared from nowhere holding a shiny Colt revolver. The hammer clicked, then slammed down on what sounded like a barrel of gunpowder. The explosion seemed to tear Ev's chest apart, shred him into a hundred lifeless pieces.

When Ev awoke sweat poured over his face. He slipped away from Susan's arm and sat up, shaking. For a moment he fought off the lingering spectre of the nightmare. When the last trace of the hideous head had dissipated, he fought to get control of his shivering arms.

The air inside the storeroom was dry and sweltering.

The thick, leathery smell of the place brought to mind the Indian lodges he'd visited as a youth. He recalled, too, the heavy aura of fear that had hung over the camp, the wild, terrified eyes of the children staring up at the band of rangers.

"Pa?" a broken voice asked as Ev sat up.

Ev peered into the dark. Todd and Rachel slept quietly. Susan rolled over, fending off some demon with one hand. Finley formed a half ball, his blond hair barely visible beneath his elbow. Leaning against the wall was Martin, his bleary eyes staring upward.

Ev got to his feet and stepped carefully around the outstretched arms and legs of the others. He finally sat down at Martin's side. The boy leaned against him, and Ev wrapped a tired arm around his son.

"You'll need your sleep tomorrow," Ev whispered.

"You will, too," Marty said.

"I had a tough time sleepin'. Must be that whack on the head Nolan gave me."

"I had a nightmare," Martin mumbled, shivering. "I never have bad dreams, Pa. Not ever."

"I had a bit of one myself, son."

"You?"

"Bein' older doesn't mean a man doesn't get scared," Ev explained. "And this, well, you don't expect someone like Nolan to ride into your house, Marty. When it happens, it. . . it. . ."

"Surprises you?"

"That's part of it. There's more, though. See, I'm used to takin' chances. I've done it before. But never with so much at risk."

"If it wasn't for us, you'd probably have taken him today," Martin said proudly.

"I don't know how. Besides, you are here, all of you."

"I never thought about it before, but I guess it's a lot harder to be old. It's easy when all you have to worry about is yourself. But when you're responsible. . ."

"That's right, son. You and I've got to look out for the others."

"And in the mornin'?" Marty asked, gazing up at his father. "What'll it be like?"

"Hard to say. I remember one time that I got myself in a mess close to this bad. I was trailin' the Fullertons, young Chad and his cousin Henry. Well, they must've had Comanche blood in 'em because they turned back on me, hid in some rocks. Fool I was, I rode right up on top of 'em. They shot my horse. Crazy animal fell on my leg, pinnin' me but good. If they'd been better shots, I wouldn't still be here. Neither would Rachel, come to think about it. That was two years before she was born."

"But you got away?" Martin asked.

"I dragged myself away. Those Fullertons must've emptied two magazines from their Winchesters. Then they rode off. I got myself up and tracked 'em. They camped right on the river, the Trinity, that is, built a fire tall as you are. I couldn't miss 'em."

"Did you shoot 'em?"

"That's not a marshal's job, Marty," Ev whispered, gripping the boy tightly as he recalled the moment. "I drew down on 'em, ordered 'em to drop their arms. They did. Then I took 'em back to Jacksboro."

"Did they hang?"

"I suppose that's the strange thing about it," Ev murmured, brushing back the sweaty hair from his face. "Judge found 'em innocent. Fined 'em for my horse, though."

"Don't suppose it'll turn out that way tomorrow, though."

"Doesn't seem likely."

Martin turned around and pried splinters of wood from one of the planks that formed the storeroom wall.

"I thought maybe I could make a hole big enough for

Todd to crawl through," Marty explained. "He and Rachel could get clear that way."

"I thought about that. Or diggin' a tunnel. But there's not much time."

"If we could only do something," Marty whispered, clawing the wood in frustration. "I feel so helpless."

"I know," Ev said, rubbing the boy's shoulders. "Promise me something, though."

"Anything, Pa."

"If the shooting starts, get clear."

"But you'll need me."

"Your ma'll need you more," Ev said somberly.

It was as close as he could come to saying good-bye.

CHAPTER 8

EV got no more than an hour or so of real rest that night. As golden streams of sunlight filtered through the cracks in the planking of the storeroom, he yawned away his weariness and sat up. Martin lay slumped against the wall a few inches away. Ev knew the boy hadn't slept much, either.

Slowly the others greeted the morning. Art Hyland rolled his rounded body over a few times, then sat up, coughing. The gambler rose slowly from his place, rubbed his wounded side and began dressing. Susan busied herself with Rachel and Todd. Ev nudged Martin to life, then picked up Finley and shook the boy awake.

"He'd sleep through a cyclone," Martin joked as Finley ignored his father's efforts to chase away the drowsiness. "I usually turn him upside down when I need him up early."

Ev nodded, then lifted the limp body by the ankles. Finley opened his mouth and made a half-howl. Then one eye popped open.

"Pa!" Finley complained, "set me down."

Ev eased the boy to the ground, then laughed as Finley glanced around the room. Todd and Rachel giggled, and even the gambler appeared amused. Finley gazed at the smiling faces with confused eyes.

"Must be those chicken legs of yours, Fin," Martin said finally. The room filled with laughter, and Finley hurriedly scrambled into his overalls.

Ev warmly touched young Finley's shoulder. The

laughter had for a moment chased away the worst of his fears, the greatest doubts.

"Guess we'd best turn our attention to the situation at hand now," the gambler said. The smiles faded from the children. Even little Todd lost his smile, and Rachel huddled in her mother's skirts.

"They'll be comin' soon," Ev said, staring through the cracks in the wall and searching the misty ground for signs of life. He saw none. The sole sound came from the woodpile. Someone was chopping kindling.

"Let's go over it one final time," the gambler said, smoothing out the dirt beside the door and motioning for Ev and Art to gather around. In the faint light the gambler sketched the house and stable. Ev added the woodpile and the path toward the water hole. Finally the gambler placed five small x's to indicate the members of Nolan's gang.

"Ev," Susan pleaded, touching him lightly on the shoulder. "Ev, please wait for the stage."

Ev gripped her hand, then turned to gaze at Martin.

"Marty, I want you to see your mother, Rachel, and the boys safely to the water hole. Promise me?"

"But, Pa," Martin objected.

Ev's eyes pleaded, and Marty nodded sadly.

"Somebody's comin'," Art said then, and Ev hugged Susan tightly. He then drew the children to him, kissing Rachel and Todd, gripping Finley and Martin firmly by the hand. No words were exchanged. Everything had been said.

As the key turned in the padlock, the gambler palmed his pistol as he no doubt had concealed many a card over the years.

"There's two of 'em," the gambler pointed out.

The door swung open then, and a smiling Rip Hazlewood stepped inside.

"Well, you're all up bright and early," Hazlewood told them, swinging his Winchester around the room. Ev and the others blinked as a flood of bright light assaulted their eyes. "Hope you slept well. This is apt to be a big day."

"More so than you think," the gambler said, revealing the pistol and pressing the barrel against Hazlewood's belly. "Now you'd agree with that, wouldn't you?"

Hazlewood's smile faded quickly, and Ev took the rifle away and passed it into Art Hyland's waiting hands.

"Why don't you invite your friend inside?" the gambler asked quietly. "Keep in mind a man dies awful slow with a hole in his middle."

Hazlewood shivered slightly, then swallowed.

"Hey, Lou," the outlaw said calmly. "You got to come in and catch a look at this."

"At what?" Stacy grumbled. "Come along, Rip. We've got no time for your prankin' this mornin'."

"Never knew you to shy away from a sight like this," Hazlewood said, regaining his composure in spite of the gambler's pistol. "Pair of legs like these, my goodness!"

"Legs, you say?" Stacy asked, laughing. "Well, I should've known."

Stacy stepped to the doorway with his rifle carried loosely under one arm. Ev took a deep breath, then reached out and pulled the former driver inside. Art grabbed the rifle, and Ev slammed an elbow across Stacy's forehead, felling the man.

"Well now, that's the first two," the gambler said, pushing Hazlewood into the far corner of the storeroom. Ev found some rope and passed it to Martin.

"You're makin' a mistake, Marshal," Hazlewood complained as Martin tied the two captives' feet and hands. "Uncle George is watchin' from the porch. He'll already be figurin' something's gone wrong."

"Then you're as dead as we are," Martin said, tightening the ropes on Hazlewood's wrists until the outlaw winced.

"They are liable to suspect something's wrong," Ev said nervously. "We'd better get goin'."

"I tell you. . ." Hazlewood began. But Marty stuffed a flour sack in the young man's mouth.

"Watch 'em," Ev told the gambler, then took one of the Winchesters and crept out the door. No one moved outside. The porch stood deserted. The gambler stepped out, too.

"Thought you were goin' to watch the others," Ev whispered.

"You think that fat driver's a match for Nolan, I'll happily go back."

Ev shook his head and waited for the gambler to start for the house. Ev then raced across the open ground toward the stable. A shot rang out from the direction of the woodpile, and Ev dove quickly as a second shot crashed into the water trough two feet away.

"One's over here, Uncle George," the clear young voice of Ben Wood called out. "Th'other's headed for the house."

"You boys best fold this hand!" Nolan yelled. "I've got all the top cards here."

"Do you?" Ev answered, firing twice toward the rifle barrel protruding from the front window of the house. The barrel vanished amid a storm of curses. Ev then burrowed himself into a depression back of the trough and edged toward the woodpile.

"I can't see him!" Nolan called out. "You, Ben?"

"I think he's out past the trough!" Ben shouted.

Ev hugged the ground as a shot missed wildly overhead. His biggest concern was for the safety of Susan and the children. He could see Marty and Finley staring out from the doorway of the storeroom. There'd been no sign of the gambler. Worse, Buck Wood was nowhere to be found.

Ev searched the scene in front of him carefully. Ben kept firing from behind the woodpile. Nolan's rifle coughed out bullets from the front door of the house.

So, it's just as you suspected, Ev told himself. Thin odds at best. If only now some glimpse could be caught of the westbound. But there was no point in hoping for help from the world beyond Antelope Springs. The isolation which had long endeared the place to Ev now worked against him. Again, as he'd been a dozen times with the rangers and a dozen more while riding down outlaws from Jacksboro, he stood alone.

What was it his father had told him, back in '59 when the Comanches had burned them out that final time? When things are at their worst, a man has to get hard, has to swallow his fear and turn it into determination. That advice had worked before, at Johnsonville and later at Selma. Now Ev would again rely upon it.

He edged forward, continuing in spite of two well-placed shots that missed by no more than a foot. He then rushed toward the stable, diving toward the wall as shots from the house split the air close by.

Now I have a chance, Ev told himself. He inched his way to the rear door of the stable, slid inside, then wove through the stalls past the horses toward the front door. The firing outside continued. Ev congratulated himself. Nolan was concentrating on the outside while Ev approached young Ben's position back of the woodpile.

"You see the marshal?" Ben called out suddenly. "I lost sight of him."

"He's not returnin' our fire," Nolan observed.

"Maybe you got him. Or he could be out of ammunition."

"Wouldn't count on that, son," Nolan said, firing again. "Get ready to move."

Ev never let the young outlaw have the opportunity. Ev

leaped forward, slamming into the neatly stacked oak logs. A cascade of firewood knocked Ben out into the open, and Ev jumped the young man.

"Uncle George!" Ben cried out as Ev slammed the Winchester against the young man's thin ribs. Ben rolled away, gasping for breath. Ev snatched the outlaw's rifle, then retreated to the protection of the stable door.

It offered scant safety, though. A rifle blasted through the roof and splintered the door. Ev dove forward as more shots splattered the woodpile. He was caught between Nolan inside the house and what was obviously Buck Wood atop the stable. Worse, Ben had managed to escape to the house, too.

"Nice try, Marshal!" Nolan shouted. "But we've got you now."

The firing continued, and Ev scrambled backward. The pile of logs offered feeble protection. Ev swung the rifle barrel out, but Buck fired immediately, clipping the woodpile only inches from Ev's left hand. He pulled back, wincing from a handful of splinters embedded in the tender flesh of his wrist.

Ev removed the splinters and tore a strip from his shirt to bind the wound. Then he tried to shoot from a different section of the woodpile. A shot from the house forced him back again.

Ev ground his teeth and crawled to the far end of the stacked logs. From there he could glimpse the storeroom. It appeared deserted.

Where's Art? Ev asked himself. What had become of the gambler? Were Susan and the children safe? He got half an answer when Marty appeared behind the chicken coop. Finley was there, too, waving frantically. Finally Ev spotted Susan and Rachel.

"Run!" Ev shouted. "Get clear."

Shots sprayed the woodpile, sending a shower of splinters down on Ev.

If only I could get to the coop, Ev thought. It's not far.

Where are you, Art? A bit of covering fire, and. . .

The rest of the answer came suddenly from the back of the house. Nolan appeared, shoving the gambler forward. The card player was unarmed. Blood covered the left side of his face. Nolan had no doubt caught him unawares.

"Well, Marshal?" Nolan asked, shoving the gambler forward and firing off two quick shots. The bullets cut through the gambler's back. For a minute the gambler spun around crazily, dropping to one knee. Ev stepped out and fired rapidly at Nolan. The outlaw'd stood in the open, grinning. But even as Ev fired, Nolan dashed away, reaching the shelter of the storeroom. Buck opened up again from the stable roof, driving Ev to shelter.

The gambler didn't die immediately. Somehow he managed to crawl forward, mumbling names, a few phrases that were muddled by cries of pain. Finally Ev noticed the stranger's eyes growing hazy. The gambler fell face down into the dust. For a moment Ev heard a kind of wheezing from the fallen man. Then there was nothing but a spreading pool of blood beside the gambler's back, a scarlet stain in the dusty earth of the station.

"Art?" Ev called out.

There was a stir inside the storeroom. The driver appeared in the doorway, only to be knocked aside by an onrushing George Nolan. Nolan's pistol barked, and Art Hyland fell sideways.

Ev fired, but again the shot was too late. He stared at the fallen bodies of his comrades, then looked at the cowering shadows that were his family. If Marty'd had a rifle. . .

No, Ev thought sadly. Courage wasn't enough to transform a fourteen-year-old into a marksman. There'd only be another corpse in the dusty ground.

"Well, Marshal?" Nolan roared again. "You still got shells for that rifle, do you?"

Ev frowned. Why hadn't he thought to drag along the rifle he'd taken from Ben? It would have taken but a minute to empty the magazine. A few more shots . . . wouldn't really matter, Ev realized.

"Run, Susan!" Ev shouted, firing at the storeroom. But though she tried, Buck fired, scattering the chickens and sending screams into the air from the direction of the coop. Ev tried to answer, but shots from the house and storeroom sent him ducking for safety. More of the same followed, sending another shower of splintered oak cascading down on Ev's head.

"He's still down there, Uncle George!" Rip Hazlewood shouted.

Hazlewood? Ev asked himself. Nolan had freed the prisoners. But why was Hazlewood shouting? If Nolan wasn't with them. . .

"Ayyyy!" a high-pitched voice screamed. Ev knew without looking that the voice belonged to Todd. It was the same terrifying cry Ev heard the night the little boy had been bitten by a cottonmouth down by the water hole. Nothing cut through a father worse than such a cry. Ev fingered the hot barrel of the rifle with fingers suddenly grown cold.

"Heh, Marshal!" Nolan called out. "Got somethin' to show you."

Ev crawled to the edge of the woodpile and reluctantly gazed toward the coop. Nolan was there, fending off Finley's attacking fists while holding Todd's kicking body securely. Light flashed off the blade of a Bowie knife held against the small boy's chest.

"Fin, get out of there!" Ev shouted, searching for some sign of Marty and the others.

"Pa?" Finley asked, stepping away as Nolan tightened his grip on Todd.

"Run!" Ev shouted.

Susan appeared then, staring at Nolan with horror-filled eyes. Behind her stood Lou Stacy, grinning as he aimed the gambler's pistol at little Rachel.

"It's over!" Nolan shouted. "Can't you see that, Marshal! Do you really want them all dead?"

"He'll do it, Marshal!" Rip Hazlewood hollered. "Give it up, now, before it's too late for them."

Ev read the deadly eyes of George Nolan, then listened as Hazlewood pleaded again.

"Toss out the rifle!" Nolan commanded.

Ev caught sight of Marty at last. The shaggy-haired boy was pulling Finley away from Nolan. Ev rose slightly so the boys could read his pleading eyes. Run, those eyes shouted. Get away. Maybe you can get help. But Finley refused to leave, and Marty wouldn't flee alone.

"Last chance, Marshal!" Nolan shouted.

Todd screamed as the knife bit into the boy's chest.

"All right!" Ev shouted, hurling the rifle out into the clearing. "I give up!"

Slowly, his knees wobbling, Ev rose to his feet. The barrels of Hazlewood's pistol and Ben's rifle fixed Ev in their sights. But Nolan waved them off.

"Let the girl go, too," Nolan told Stacy.

Ev watched as Rachel raced to her mother. Finley clung to Marty's side as Ev stepped forward.

"Got to give you this, Marshal," Nolan said, holding Todd tightly. "You did your share. If you'd had a little help, maybe we'd all be shut up in that storeroom. But you ought to've known better than to call a full house with pair of deuces."

"Let the boy go," Ev said. "You've won."

"Oh, I never doubted that," Nolan said. "But you don't expect me to forget all this, do you? Ben's got a ringin' in his ears, and Stacy there's got a busted rib or two."

"So, I'm here," Ev said, holding his empty hands out. "What's stoppin' you?"

"Actually," Nolan said, "it doesn't appear to do much good crackin' you on the head. I could shoot you, but then who'd greet the stage? No, I guess you'd say I'm short on choices. But maybe if we did a little carvin' on this boy. . ."

Nolan pricked Todd's ear with the knife. The boy kept his lip stiff, and except for a slight shiver, Todd remained still.

"If you harm that boy, I'll see you dead," Ev promised, glaring at Nolan with fiery eyes.

"Will you now?" Nolan said, pricking Todd's ear a second time.

"Uncle George!" Hazlewood pleaded. "The stage could be here any minute."

"Guess it might be hard for the marshal to convince the driver all's well when he's got blood runnin' down his arm. And we did leave the place a little cluttered," Nolan added, pointing to the gambler's shattered body.

"Myself, I'd feel better with a little breakfast," Hazlewood said, turning to Susan. "Bacon and eggs, maybe?"

"Yes," Susan said, hugging Rachel to her as she started toward the house. "Todd, fetch the eggs."

Todd gazed upward into Nolan's cold eyes. The outlaw relaxed his grip, and Todd scurried away.

"Rip, you figure you can get the rest of these folks back into the storeroom?" Nolan asked. "If not, I'll tend to 'em myself."

Hazlewood frowned, then waved the pistol at Ev.

"Marshal Raymond won't be givin' anybody trouble for a while," Ben said, waving a Winchester at Susan.

Nolan chuckled, then started toward the house. As he passed Art Hyland, he gave the driver a sharp kick. Art groaned, and Nolan kicked a second time.

"Him, too, Rip." Nolan ordered. "Drag the gambler inside the stable. Give the marshal a fresh shirt and some water to clean himself up with."

Ev shoveled Marty and Fin along in front of him, then helped Art up. The driver clutched a bleeding shoulder and staggered through the door.

"He'll need some bandages," Ev told Hazlewood.

"He's lucky not to be dead," Hazlewood answered. "You, too. Next time you might not get off so easy."

Ev nodded as the door swung shut. He helped Art to the ground, then turned to gaze through the cracks. Susan and Rachel drifted through the back door of the house. Todd followed, holding eggs in his hat.

"Pa?" Martin said, touching Ev's bloody wrist.

"I know, son," Ev said, drawing Marty to him with one hand and Finley with the other. "I know."

CHAPTER 9

WHILE Susan fried bacon and scrambled eggs for Nolan's men, Ev did his best to treat Art Hyland's wounded shoulder. There was no hope of removing the bullet, not in the faint light of the storeroom. And besides, Ev had no knife. The best he could do was tear strips from his shirt and bind the damaged shoulder.

"At least I got the bleedin' stopped," Ev said, easing Art's head onto a piece of canvas Martin had rolled into a pillow.

"I'll be dead in a week if that bullet's left in there," Art complained. "I've seen it before, the festerin' and the fever."

"You could be dead right now," Ev told him. "I can't for the life of me understand how Nolan could've missed that belly of yours."

"He didn't miss the gambler," Marty said from the far wall. "Never gave him a chance."

"It was his choice," Ev said, rejoining the boys. "All his life he bet on his luck. This time he lost."

For a few minutes they sat together beside the door, reflecting on the failed attempt to overpower Nolan. Then the sound of footsteps approaching from the house attracted their attention. A key turned in the padlock, and the door swung open.

This time Hazlewood remained safely outside, in plain view from Buck Wood's vantage point atop the stable. Todd and Rachel stumbled through the doorway, followed by Susan. She carried with her the promised shirt and a bucket of water. Once Hazlewood closed the door,

Todd drew slices of bread from beneath his shirt. Rachel'd smuggled some butter, and Susan had hidden a half pound of smoked ham under the shirt.

"I have to admit to bein' a little hungry myself," Ev said as he eyed the food. "Thirsty, too."

"We all are," Susan said, setting down the meat, then taking out a sharp carving knife.

"That might be useful," Ev said as she carved the ham. "How'd you manage to pick that up without anyone noticin'?"

"I don't suppose they think we'll try anything else," she said, patting him on the knee. "Or maybe they don't think I'd have the nerve. Rip Hazlewood was watching me in the kitchen, but he seemed more interested in helping Todd and Rachel with the plates than in keeping an eye on me."

"He's tryin' to ease his conscience," Ev said, frowning. "He's a strange one. He comes in here, betrays us, then the next day stops Nolan from hurtin' Todd."

"Maybe he'll help us escape," Martin said. "I'll ask him."

"You watch yourself, Martin Raymond," Susan warned as she handed the first slice of ham and bread to Ev. "I wouldn't trust any of those men."

"She's right," Ev said, passing the food along to Finley. "None of us are out of here yet."

"We won't be, either," Martin said, sinking his face into his hands.

"Don't forget, son. They haven't robbed the westbound yet," Ev reminded them. "We'll have another chance."

Susan's hand shook, and she almost sliced her finger instead of the ham.

"Enough of that talk," she declared. "Let's have something to eat, get you cleaned up."

Ev nodded. After distributing the rest of the food, Ev knelt beside Art Hyland as they shared a short prayer.

"Lord, deliver us from our oppressors," Susan prayed. "Watch over us."

Ev had never relied much on prayers, but just then he joined Susan's thoughts with all his heart. Afterward, he tried to convince Art to eat something. The big man refused the ham, though, accepting only some water and a crust of bread.

After the food had been devoured, Ev washed his chest and arm, then let Susan wrap his wrist with strips torn from an old kerchief. He felt better wearing a clean shirt, and the sting from his wrist died away. But as the day wore on, the room grew increasingly warm. Ev was greatly relieved when the door swung open, and Rip Hazlewood motioned them outside.

"No, not the little ones," Hazlewood said, pointing to Todd and Rachel. "You best stay as well, Mrs. Raymond. Don't believe you'd be of much use."

"For what?" Ev asked, blocking Martin and Finley from leaving.

"Well, it's gettin' a bit warm, Marshal," Hazlewood explained. "That gambler, well, he's startin' to smell. Uncle George says you'd best put him in the ground. Wouldn't want the stage warned."

"Bury him yourself," Martin said angrily. "You killed him."

"That's not bein' cooperative, Marty," Hazlewood said, smiling at the boy. "Truth is, Marshal, I figured you wouldn't mind the air. I'll leave the door open while you're outside, let the others catch the breeze. I'll even let you fetch a fresh bucket of water."

"Ev," Susan said, staring up at her husband with pleading eyes. "There's Art to think of, too."

Yes, Ev thought. She can take the bullet out while we're outside.

"You'll guard them yourself?" Ev asked.

"That's right. Ben and Lou Stacy'll be with you."

Ev frowned. Wasn't likely he could get Marty and Fin past young Ben. Stacy'd be on his guard, too.

"We got this settled?" Hazlewood asked.

Ev nodded, and Hazlewood stepped away from the door. Ev led the older boys outside where they were escorted to the barn by Ben Wood.

"There he is," Ben said, pointing to the lifeless gambler. "Uncle George said to bury him out back, past the stable."

"There's a shady spot above the springs," Ev pointed out. "Would that be all right?"

"Suit yourself," Ben said, shrugging his shoulders. "Seems far to carry him, but maybe the ground's softer. You're diggin' the hole."

"He was a good man," Marty said, lifting one of the dead man's legs as Fin grabbed the other. "He deserves a proper grave."

"Don't expect it matters much to him," Ben joked.

Ev ignored the comment and lifted the man's shoulders. The stench was awful, and Ben gave them a wide berth. Ev and the boys carried the body past the stable, past the springs, and on to where two live oaks stood on the crest of a small hill. Lou Stacy appeared with a spade, and Ev started the digging.

"I'll get another spade," Marty said, starting for the barn.

"Hold on there," Stacy called, intercepting the boy. "One spade's enough. There's only one grave to dig. . . so far. A spade makes a fair-to-middlin' club. I believe we'll just allow you to take turns, Ev, you and the boys."

"It'll take longer that way," Marty warned.

"I've got time," Stacy replied.

"The westbound could come along any time now," Ev said as he continued digging. "It'd be best they didn't happen along while we're buryin' him."

"Then you best get on with it," Ben said, kicking a stone toward Ev. "I'm not so well disposed toward you as Rip,

Marshal. I'd as soon shoot the all of you and get along with things."

Ev glared at Ben. If Ev'd wanted, he might have killed the young man that morning. Ben seemed to feel the anger directed his way. The young outlaw drew out his pistol and kept it handy.

Ev had the grave well started when Marty volunteered to take over.

"Sure you know what to do?" Ev asked the boy.

"I've dug lots of holes, Pa. Graves aren't so different, are they?"

Martin then stripped off his shirt and took the spade. As Marty dug, Ev smiled with approval. Marty's back was broadening, and his leathery shoulders were losing their boyish roundness.

I just hope he has a chance to grow older, Ev thought, sitting beside Finley.

"Pa?" Finley said, leaning on Ev's shoulder.

"You all right, son?" Ev asked.

"Pa, I never saw anybody dead before," Finley said, pointing sadly at the gambler's body. "He's awful cold and stiff."

Ev nodded, then pulled the twelve-year-old closer.

"It's like that skunk you shot last winter. Just the same."

"No, it's different with a man," Ev said. "A man ought to have words read over him."

"Will somebody read words over me, Pa?"

"That's not goin' to happen for a long time yet," Ev said, hugging the boy. Ev felt tears drop on his shoulder, and he wished there was some way to fend off the terror. There wasn't.

"I wanted to run away," Finley whispered.

"I wish you had. You're a mighty fine runner, Finley Raymond. You might've gotten to the Merritt place."

"I could've brought help," he mumbled.

"That wasn't why I wanted you to go."

"I know," Finley said, crawling up Ev's knee as he'd done when smaller. "But this way I can help you."

"Sure can," Ev said, holding him tightly.

A few moments later Finley took a brief turn at the digging. The spade was heavy for his small arms to handle, though, and the ground was rocky and hard.

"I think it's my time again," Ev finally said, taking over. Ev dug the grave deeper. Three feet down he ran into solid rock.

"That's deep enough anyhow," Stacy declared. "Let's toss him in and get done with this."

"You've got to read words over him," Finley said, jumping up. "Pa says so."

"We're not doin' things his way," Ben declared.

Ev motioned Finley back to the trees, then shoveled the remaining dirt from the shallow trench. As Ev climbed out of the grave, Stacy kicked the gambler's body into the hole.

"Now cover him up," Stacy ordered.

"We ought to at least give him a moment of respect," Ev said, waving the boys over. The outlaws stood silently as Ev and his sons bowed their heads.

"I wish I remembered some of my Bible verses," Martin said, gripping Ev's hand tightly.

"We don't even know his name," Finley added with a sigh.

"I remember what my father said when we laid my brother Palmer in the ground," Ev said. "Hold him close, Lord."

"You finished?" Stacy asked, kicking dirt into the grave. "Cover him up. We've got things to attend to."

Ev took the spade and began filling the hole. Martin slipped on the shirt, then helped Finley line the grave with stones.

"Later I'll carve a marker, Pa," Finley promised.

"I think he'd like that, son," Ev said, patting the boy's back.

"We ever goin' to finish with this?" Stacy asked.

"A man's buryin' ought to take a moment or two," Ev replied angrily.

The outlaws laughed, then took the spade and hurriedly filled in the grave. Stacy delighted in kicking away the stones Finley had placed. But Ev said nothing, just waited for Stacy and young Ben to finish.

"We'll all end up on that hill," Marty whispered as they returned to the storeroom. "They'll kill us all."

"Maybe not, son," Ev said somberly. "The could just ride away, leave us locked in the storeroom."

"No," Marty said.

When they were locked away in their one-room prison again, Ev embraced Susan, touched Todd and Rachel on their heads, then checked on Art Hyland.

"I got the bullet out," Susan explained, "but it was deep. I'm afraid he'll bleed to death. This heat won't do him any good, either."

"You did what you could," Ev told her.

"Not much comfort in that."

"Pa," Martin said then, tugging at Ev's hand.

"Yes, son?" Ev answered.

"Can we talk a bit?"

"Sure," Ev agreed, following Martin to the far side of the room.

"Pa, you remember that pistol Tom Shipley offered me back in March?" Martin asked.

"The one I said you couldn't buy?" Ev asked.

"That's the one," Martin said. He hesitated. "I know I shouldn't have let him, but Tom said he didn't have any use for it, and I figured you might change your mind."

"So you took the pistol?"

"Yes, sir," Martin admitted, dropping his head. "Tom

wouldn't leave any shells for the gun, not with your disapprovin', but he did leave the gun."

"Nolan's likely found it by now," Ev explained. "He turned the house upside down. Even if he didn't, an empty gun isn't much use."

"They wouldn't've found the gun," Marty said. "I hid it good so you wouldn't find it."

"Where?"

"In the stable."

"You mean it's in that cigar box you keep by the back door?"

"You know about that, Pa?"

"I stumbled across it a while back," Ev confessed.

"You didn't look inside, did you?" Martin asked, shifting his weight from one foot to the other, then back again.

"I figure you're entitled to your secrets," Ev told the boy. "So, the gun's likely still there."

"I know the gun's empty, Pa, but when Rip was in here, Art took his gunbelt. While all the shootin' was goin' on, I helped myself."

Martin reached into the same flour barrel in which Ev had hidden the gambler's pistol. Inside a small leather pouch were fourteen shells.

"All I had time to take," Martin explained. "I was thinkin' that they wouldn't get too suspicious if you went into the stable. You could load the gun, then surprise 'em when the stage arrives."

"Maybe," Ev agreed.

"It'd give us a chance, Pa."

"It might at that. And while I've got Nolan occupied, you might get your brothers and sister down the hill. Marty, do you remember that cave in the rocks past the water hole?"

"Sure."

"You'll be safe there. You won't have time to pause,

though. Nobody'll be watching you. Carry Rachel if you
have to, but head out in a hurry."

"How long should we stay there?"

"Till I come and get you," Ev said, gripping the boy's
shoulder. "Or until someone else does."

"I'm not a boy anymore, you know," Marty said. "I
should stay and help. Fin can. . ."

"Can carry Rachel? No, I'd feel better if you were with
them, son. Truth is, you've got the hardest job of all. You
have to hide out and wait, look after your brothers and
sister. You won't know what's happening, and you can't
leave to find out."

"Pa?"

"No matter what else happens, Marty, it's important you
children are safe. You understand?"

"Yes, sir," Martin said sadly.

Ev squeezed the boy's shoulder. Martin's chin fell, and
Ev lifted it as he had a thousand times before.

"Cheer up, Marty," Ev said. "You've given us all a
chance."

But in spite of Ev's words and his smiles, Martin's eyes
clouded with misgivings. And Ev found himself praying
again, hoping somehow he'd have a chance to protect his
family after all, to give shaggy-haired Marty and thin Finley, little Todd, and precious Rachel a chance to grow
taller and older.

Maybe I'll even be able to get Susan away, Ev told himself. He hoped and prayed and dreamed of it. The idea
brightened his eyes, gave him the strength to endure those
next few hours.

CHAPTER 10

IT was difficult to judge the passage of time, locked inside the storeroom as Ev was. Still, it couldn't have been much past midday when George Nolan ordered the door opened.

"You had time to think on that gambler?" the outlaw leader asked. "Well, Marshal, you considered how it'd be if that was one of your young ones down there in that hole? Because next time you send trouble my way, it will be."

"I've done my thinkin'," Ev said bitterly.

"Then it's time you rejoined us," Nolan said, pointing the way toward the stable. Ev slipped out the door, followed by Martin, Finley, and Susan. Before the little ones could exit, Nolan motioned them all to stop.

"Rip, who'd you say'd be outside?" Nolan asked.

"Well, Uncle George, only ones I saw when you boys rode up were the marshal, Marty, and young Fin. Mrs. Raymond and the girl were inside as I recall."

"Then you stay in there," Nolan told Susan, shoving her backward so that she lost her balance and fell to the ground.

"Keep your hands off her!" Ev yelled, rushing to Susan's side.

"I'm all right," Susan assured him as Ev helped her up. "Go on. We'll be fine."

Ev glared angrily at Nolan, but the outlaw's icy stare stopped any words from being spoken.

"You look after your ma now, Todd," Ev said instead. "You, too, Rachel."

The youngsters nodded. Hazlewood shut the door and locked it. Ev followed Nolan toward the stable, flanked by Martin and Finley.

"What would you be doin' about now normally?" Nolan asked.

"Mendin' a harness maybe," Ev said. "Workin' the horses."

Martin headed toward the ready corral, but Ben blocked the way.

"That's right, boy," Nolan said. "You stay clear of that corral. I'd sure hate for you to make the same mistake twice, let those ponies out. Kept us busy quite a while roundin' 'em up. If it was to happen again, I might not believe it was an accident. Might even have to ask Buck to do a little shootin'.'"

"You believe what you want to," Marty said, spitting about an inch from Ben's boot.

"That wasn't friendly at all," Ben said, swinging his rifle so that the stock landed squarely against Martin's back. The boy fell forward, landing hard on his hands.

"Marty!" Ev shouted as Martin turned around, ready to pounce on Ben. "It's not the time, son! Not the time!"

"When will it be?" Martin asked, his eyes blazing.

"Never," Nolan said, laughing at them. "Can't say we really need you just now, boy. You make another move toward Ben, we'll be diggin' another grave."

Ben's smile broadened, and Marty drew back. Ben's fingers seemed eager to fire the Winchester.

"Marty," Finley said, pulling his brother away toward the stable. "He'd shoot you sure."

"You believe that," Ben snapped. "'Fore you got within ten feet."

"Now get on with your chores!" Nolan shouted. "I want things to look normal-like when the westbound arrives. You boys stack those logs like before. Marshal, you pull out the harness. Make like you're mendin' it."

"It needs mendin'," Marty said, motioning toward the inside of the stable. "You remember that piece I was tellin' you about, Pa, those leaders I put up special. Inside."

Ev nodded. Marty meant the gun. Ev had no intention of letting Nolan discover that pistol before the stage appeared. There was no point in taking the gun back to the storeroom or carrying it. If discovered, it'd get someone killed, and the outlaws weren't likely to offer another chance to be jumped while opening the door.

Still, Ev thought as he entered the stable, the pistol could be loaded, the spare bullets stashed with the gun. Maybe he could hide it somewhere so that when needed, it would be easier to get.

Ev glanced behind him. Lou Stacy was watching from the doorway, but the ex-driver paid little attention. Ev picked up a section of harness that could use work, then continued toward Marty's hiding place. Ev drew the gun from the cigar box and concealed it under the harness. Stacy never suspected a thing. Once back outside, Ev spread out the harness and carefully slid the gun under one knee as he sat beside the woodpile.

"That looks just fine," Nolan said, as Martin and Finley restacked logs. "All seems well."

"There's no fire in the chimney," Hazlewood noted.

"Too hot this hour of the day," Ev said.

"Marshal's bein' clever," Hazlewood said. "I remember Mrs. Raymond mostly did her baking 'round this time of the mornin'. I'll put a couple of logs on."

"You do that, Rip," Nolan said. "See, Marshal, I trained that boy right."

"Taught him all you know, huh?" Ev asked. "This way he can end up swingin' from a rope's end same as you."

"I wouldn't be too sure who's apt to end up on the short end of a rope if I was you, Marshal," Nolan retorted. "Whatever comes of Rip, you're not likely to be around to know."

"Pa?" Finley asked, nervously grabbing Ev's arm.

"It hasn't happened yet," Ev said.

"No, but it will," Nolan promised.

"Don't give him much thought, Fin," Ev said, turning the boy's head away from Nolan. "The thing to do is stack those logs, get 'em lined up proper like they were before Nolan arrived. It'll take your mind off things."

Finley nodded and set his mind to the task. Martin picked up slivers of wood and carried them cautiously to the kindling box on the porch of the house. Ev lifted the harness onto one shoulder, then quietly began loading bullets into the six chambers of the pistol. When he'd finished, he set the gun and the spare bullets atop the woodpile. Martin placed a log on top, concealing the weapon from all but the most careful examination.

"It'll need some tools to mend this harness properly," Ev announced then.

"No tools!" Nolan yelled. "You don't have to mend it. You just look like that's what you're doin'. Understand?"

Ev nodded. It seemed a pure waste of time, but it probably didn't matter. He felt good knowing Nolan was worried about the tools. Maybe that way there'd be little suspicion a gun was hidden close by.

"What should we do now, Pa?" Finley asked as Martin set the last stray log atop the pile.

Before Ev could answer, Buck shouted from the roof.

"I see dust, Uncle George!" the lookout called out. "From over there!"

Ev turned and stared as Buck pointed toward the water hole.

"That's not the east," Nolan declared. "Ever see a stage come up that way, Rip?"

"Never," Hazlewood said, stepping out from the house to have a second look.

"That's where I stashed the stage," Stacy said nervously.

"Anybody live out that way, Marshal?" Nolan asked.

Ev turned back to the harness, but the sound of a Colt's hammer clicking forced a response.

"I bought this place from Bill Merritt," Ev explained. "He owns all that land back there."

"He ride out often?"

"Once or twice a month," Ev replied. "Sometimes one of his boys comes by. Aren't many kids in this country."

"I'll ride out and stop him," Marty offered.

"No, you won't," Nolan said, stepping off the porch. "I don't want some neighbor raisin' the whole county against us. You keep whoever it is in your sights, Bucky. We'll let him come along in."

Ev felt his legs wobble as he envisioned Bill Merritt riding in, getting himself shot. But as the rider came closer, it was clearly not Bill.

"It's Tim," Martin said, turning to Ev with a fearful look in his eyes. "Pa, what'll we do?"

"Nothing," Ev said, nodding to where Lou Stacy stood beside the storeroom. Buck was above them, his rifle trained toward the visitor. Ben and Rip Hazlewood huddled behind George Nolan in the shadows of the house. A single cry, a hurried warning, and a burst of gunfire would follow.

"Pa?" Martin asked again.

Ev shook his head sadly and watched as young Tim Merritt approached. Tim's hair was as fine and fair as Finley's, and his face had always been thin. Although Martin's age, Tim was small, somewhat frail like his mother. Behind Tim's broad-backed brown mare trailed Star, the mustang pony Marty had released from the corral.

It's like Tim Merritt to have brought that horse in, Ev told himself. Like as not, he's worried Martin's in trouble. Well, he is, Ev realized. But so are you, Tim.

"Hey, Mr. Raymond, lookee what I come across!" Tim

shouted, waving his hat in the air with one hand and holding the rope with which he'd captured Star in the other. "Bet you thought Star was halfway to tomorrow!"

"Guess. . . I lost track of him," Martin said, trying to conceal his fear.

"Got a lot of company?" Tim asked. "I guess they came back here once the stage went off the trail. I saw it on my way over. Pa'll be glad to help right her."

Nolan swung his pistol around and motioned for Ev to say something.

"Thanks," Ev said. "You don't have to come any farther. Marty can come out and get the horse."

"You got sickness or somethin'?" Tim asked, halting his horse and gazing warily toward the station. "Everything all right, Mr. Raymond?"

"Just fine," Ev said. "How's your mother?"

"Busy bakin'," Tim said, examining the corral. "Westbound not here yet? I see you've got a team ready."

"Tell him to shut up and clear out," Stacy said quietly. "Get rid of him."

"No, invite him to supper," Nolan said, stepping out into the clear. "Go on, Marshal."

"We appreciate you bringin' the horse back, Tim," Ev said, starting toward where Tim had stopped a hundred and fifty feet away. "But I expect you've got chores waitin' for you at home."

"I've got time," Tim said, noticing first Nolan, then Lou Stacy. "You drivin' the stage again now, Mr. Stacy?"

"Now and then," Stacy lied.

"Never knew you to keep a rifle so handy," Tim declared. "Marty, you sure everything's all right? I don't smell bread. Your ma's always bakin' bread midweek."

"Get him on in here, Marshal!" Nolan ordered.

"I know you're in a hurry, Tim," Ev said.

"But we're about to have our lunch," Nolan interrupted. "Boy like you's bound to be hungry. Wouldn't be neighborly not to reward your kindness in returnin' that horse."

"Who're you?" Tim asked. "What's that in your hand?"

Tim's face grew pale as he realized Nolan held a pistol. The boy turned his horse and kicked it into a gallop.

"Buck!" Nolan shouted, and before Ev had time to yell a warning, the Winchester atop the stable cracked twice. Young Tim Merritt spun sideways from his horse and fell into the dust. The two horses raced wildly away, whining in terror. Martin stepped back in horror, and Finley hid his face in the woodpile. Ev glared defiantly at Nolan and walked slowly forward.

"Hold on there, Marshal!" Nolan said, firing his pistol into the ground a foot ahead of Ev.

"He's no threat to you now!" Ev shouted. "I'm going to him."

"Marshal, he'll shoot!" Hazlewood warned.

"Let him," Ev said, marching. "If he's bound to do it, let him. I'm tired of listenin' to orders. There's a boy out there who's done nothin' to anybody 'cept round up a stray horse and bring it home. Now he's lyin' out there in the dust."

"Let him go," Stacy said. He chuckled. "Buck doesn't miss, George. You know that. We've got the kids, the woman. Marshal won't do anything stupid, will you, Ev?"

Ignoring Stacy altogether, Ev walked to where Tim Merritt's still body lay. He could feel Nolan's angry eyes burning through his back. The pistol was still cocked, no doubt. Any second a shot might ring out, ending the nightmare once and for all. But somehow it just didn't matter anymore.

What am I going to do? Ev asked himself as he knelt beside Tim's motionless shoulders. One shot had clearly shattered the boy's right arm. The other had done the real harm, though, slamming through the fourteen-year-old's chest. Tim's still, lifeless blue eyes stared skyward, filled with confusion. Why? they seemed to be asking.

"Why?" Ev asked aloud, gently closing the lids, then lifting the limp, blood-soaked body. "Why?" he asked again as he headed back to the house.

"I'll never forget what you've done!" Martin shouted, staring at Rip Hazelwood in particular. "You're murderers!"

Marty glanced momentarily at the woodpile, but Ev's eyes warned the boy away.

"We can't even take him home, Pa," Marty said, his face overcome with grief. "God, Pa, they killed him!"

"Should've brought him on in like I said," Nolan said, walking toward Ev. "Could've thrown him into the storeroom with the rest of you."

"No, I saw your eyes!" Martin said, shaking from head to toe. "You meant to kill him."

"It happens," Nolan said, reaching over and touching Tim's bloody chest. "Not much bigger'n a flea, this one, Rip. Want to have a look?"

"Stay away," Ev roared, angrily backing from Nolan's outstretched hand. "You're not fit to touch him, Nolan!"

"Why?" Nolan asked, pointing his pistol at Ev's head. "'Cause I don't have a badge? I've seen plenty of dead men. Boys, too."

"Like at Gainesville?"

"Red River Crossing, too. Before that up the Trinity a ways. People ought to be more careful. They get in the way, they get shot."

"Lots of people get in your way, don't they?" Ev raged. "I hope to God someday you find yourself facin' a jury of twelve men who've got sons Tim's age. You'll see justice done then."

"Sure will," Ben mocked. "I'm scared already, aren't you, Uncle George?"

Nolan, too, snickered. Ev turned away, though. He laid Tim's corpse inside the stable and covered it with a saddle blanket. For a second, Ev thought he would become sick. But the anger swallowed his nausea. He looked down at the lump beneath the blanket, at the bit of blond hair at the top and saw Finley, then little Todd. Fury boiled up inside him, and he wanted—needed to strike out at something, anything.

"Pa?" Marty asked with equally wild eyes. The boy pointed toward the woodpile again, toward the gun that would exact a price for a murdered boy.

"It's not the right time," Ev said, choking on the words. What would be the right time, when Marty and Fin, Todd and Rachel, Susan and Ev himself lay bleeding and dying? When would Nolan and the others start to pay?

"It's time you came on out of there, Marshal," Nolan said. "You can bury the boy after we eat."

"Eat?" Marty gasped. "Eat? You can eat after. . ."

"I can always eat," Nolan said, rubbing his belly. "Fetch the woman, Lou, and bring the others in, too. We'll have ourselves a family meal."

Ev felt his legs go numb. He had to lean against Martin to keep from falling.

"Pa?" Marty asked again, clutching at Ev with both hands while Finley leaned his head against Ev's ribs.

"Try to cast it from your mind, boys," Ev said hoarsely as they made their way toward the storeroom. But deep down Ev knew it wasn't possible. There'd be nightmares that night. If there was a night.

"Ev?" Susan whispered to him as Hazlewood opened the door.

"I know," he said, holding onto the boys tightly as they entered the storeroom. "Now none of us is safe."

CHAPTER 11

THEY didn't remain in the storeroom for long. Lou Stacy came to take Susan into the kitchen.

"Come along, Rachel," Susan told her daughter, but Stacy shook his head.

"Just you," Stacy declared. "We'll send for the rest of them when the time comes."

As the door slammed shut, Ev rocked Rachel on his knee and waved Todd closer.

"How's Art?" Ev asked.

"Still sleepin'," Todd said. "Ma says he's got a fever. We give him water when he wakes up."

As best he could tell in the darkness, Ev didn't think the bleeding had resumed. But Art would prove to be little help.

"I hate this waitin' around," Marty said, slamming his fist against the wall. "When will they come for the rest of us?"

"They'll come when they're ready," Ev said, hugging Rachel tighter as the little girl started to whimper. "Won't be so long, though."

"We've got to bury Tim, too," Finley said sadly.

"Yeah," Martin agreed, sighing as he sat at Ev's elbow. "It's all my fault, you know."

"Your fault?" Ev asked.

"If I hadn't let Star go, Tim might never've come. It's cause of me he rode up here all alone. I might as well've shot the rifle myself."

"That's crazy," Ev replied sternly. "You did what you

thought best. You tried to get help. Don't forget, Tim saw the stage, too."

"But if he hadn't seen Star, he might've come with his pa, maybe brought some others."

"And you think it would have been different?" Ev asked. "These men are killers, son. The only difference would have been more men killed. You saw how fast Buck fired that rifle. A Winchester can get fifteen shots off. He'd as easily have killed five, six men. Us, too."

"I can't help feelin' responsible," Marty whimpered.

"I know," Ev replied. "I do, too. But it's wrong. We're not the ones who rode in here, tore up the house, shot that gambler and young Tim. It's George Nolan who's at fault. Remember that. Nolan's to blame."

"I will."

"I want you to think about something, all of you," Ev said, setting Rachel on the floor and gathering the others around. "I want you to remember that cave we talked about before. Sometime soon, maybe when the stage pulls in, you'll have a chance to get away. I want you to take it, run like March hares down the hill, past the water hole, and to that cave. Hide there. Don't come out, no matter what."

"I'm scared, though," Rachel said. "They'll shoot us."

"They'll have other things on their minds," Ev told her. "Rachel, I want you to grab hold of Martin's hand. Or Finley's. Whichever is closest. You do what they say, understand?"

Rachel nodded, and Ev turned to Todd.

"Son, I want you to run like thunder. Don't wait for the others. You know the way. Get down there first. Take the water bucket with you if you can. Fill it from the spring, the one just past the cave entrance."

"Yes, sir," Todd said, touching Ev's chest with fingers suddenly grown cold and damp. "What about food?"

"We'll see if we can smuggle some out after lunch. Now,

Fin, Marty, you boys look after the little ones, make sure Rachel gets there even if you have to carry her. Once you're safe, stay put. If you run short of food or water, wait for nightfall. You can visit the spring. Maybe you can raid the garden if you're in real need. It'd be safer to stay hidden, though."

"What if they find us?" Finley asked.

"Let's not worry about things that may not happen," Ev said, fending off the image of his children caught by Nolan's men in the open. The thought of carrying Rachel or Todd back to the stable as he'd carried Tim Merritt was too much to bear.

"We'll do it, Pa," Martin spoke for the others. "When, though?"

"You'll know, Marty," Ev assured the boy. "They rarely even notice you. First chance you have, take it."

The boys nodded, and little Rachel crawled back up Ev's knee.

"I wish you and Ma could come, too," she whispered.

"Me, too," Ev told her.

Shortly thereafter the door sprang open, and Rip Hazlewood motioned them outside.

"What's wrong with him?" Hazlewood asked when Art didn't respond.

"You forget?" Marty asked bitterly. "You shot him!"

"Not me, Marty," Rip said, shrinking backward. "But I guess it'd be best to leave him there."

"We might refill the water bucket," Ev suggested. "Maybe we could bring him something back from the kitchen?"

Hazlewood nodded, and Martin grabbed the bucket and dashed to the pump behind the kitchen. Ev half expected Marty to continue on down the hillside, leaving Ev to deal only with Hazlewood in order to assure the children's escape. But Marty returned in short order with the bucket full. After setting it inside the door, Marty stepped aside while Hazlewood secured the door.

"Now, who's hungry?" Hazlewood asked cheerfully. "I'll bet you are, Fin. How about little Rachel? You hungry, honey?"

Rachel stepped away from Hazlewood's outstretched hand, and Marty shielded Todd and Fin.

"Not bein' too friendly today, are you, Marty?" Hazlewood asked.

"What do you expect?" Martin asked, his eyes burning with hatred. "You come in here, take over my house, throw us in the storeroom, shoot my best friend!"

"That wasn't my doin', son." He shook his head.

"I'm not your son!" Marty shouted. "Never say that to me. You're not a tenth the man my pa is! Not your doin', you say? You were the one that sent them down on us! You, with your lyin' stories about cousins headin' north to buy a ranch! You're the worst one of all. At least your uncle doesn't pretend to be somethin' different!"

"Marty?" Hazlewood pleaded. "You don't understand."

"He understands just fine," Ev snapped, waving for the children to continue toward the house. "We all understand."

"Marshal. . ." Hazlewood began. But Ev's hard eyes silenced any other words that might have been spoken. They walked through the kitchen door and made their way together into the dining room. There Susan had tin plates filled with cold meat and bread. Coffee heated in the fireplace.

"Everything all right?" Susan whispered as she took her place beside Ev at the table. "I heard shouting."

Ev nodded, then bowed his head as Susan prepared to say grace.

"No need of that," Nolan growled as he stuffed a slice of ham into his mouth. "Let's get on with it."

Ev didn't flinch, and the children remained silent as

Susan spoke her prayer. Hazlewood dropped his chin, too.

"What's this, Rip?" Nolan jeered. "These farmers makin' a churchgoer out of you?"

"Maybe," Hazlewood said.

"Never knew you to go to meetin', cousin," Buck joked. "I remember the time we dumped that preacher off the ferry down south. Was your idea, as I recall."

Hazlewood avoided Martin's eyes.

"Maybe he's feelin' guilty," Martin said. "Over Tim."

"That boy?" Nolan asked through a mouthful of food. "That young cub we shot?"

"Not everybody has an easy time living with such a thing," Susan said. "There's no excuse. . ."

"Excuse!" Nolan shouted, pounding his hand on the table. "Excuse? We make no excuses. We do what we have to." He tossed his plate against the wall. "We do what we want, *when* we want!"

Susan's face grew pale as Nolan stormed about the room, upsetting a table here, kicking a chair there.

"I'll get you another plate, Uncle George," Hazlewood offered.

"No, let him fetch it," Nolan yelled, pointing at Martin. "Let young Mr. High and Mighty do a little work."

"I'll watch him," Ben volunteered.

"No, he can tend it on his own, can't he, Marshal?" Nolan asked.

"He could take off out the back door," Stacy pointed out.

"No, not that one," Nolan jeered. "He'll be back. He doesn't want anything to happen to his ma and pa. He wouldn't want his little bit of a brother to lose half an ear."

Todd shuddered, and Susan glared.

"I'll get it," Martin said. "You wouldn't understand a thing like loyalty, would you? You'd run the second you left the room."

"You know it," Nolan said. He grinned as he sat down again. "In this life, a man looks to his own interests. He stays alive that way."

"Is he right, Rip?" Martin asked.

"Right as rain," Hazlewood said, sadly staring down at his food.

"I hope when your time comes, you'll die alone, off by yourself in some tangle of briars," Martin said, halting in the doorway. "I hope you find yourself off in the night with a dozen wolves snappin' at your heels. I hope. . ."

"That's enough, Marty!" Susan shouted. "Get another plate."

Martin silently turned away and found a plate. After setting it in front of Nolan, Susan filled it with food. Marty sat down and picked at his food.

After eating, Ev helped Susan scrub the plates. The children busied themselves cleaning the dining room. It hadn't taken Nolan's men long to undo the last cleaning. Finally Nolan ordered everyone out front.

"Won't be much longer till the stage arrives," the outlaw told them. "I want no repeat of this mornin'. You watch yourselves, and everybody'll get through this in one piece. Otherwise, I'll start cuttin' notches in ears."

Ev nodded.

"Now, Marshal, that boy seemed bothered by the horses. Anything wrong there?" Nolan asked.

"He saw the stage," Ev explained. "There should've been another team in the corral. The westbound won't see it. They'd be worried if there were two teams there and no other coach."

"Anyone else likely to happen by?" Nolan asked.

"Could be," Ev said dourly. "Tim's folks'll worry."

"Keep a sharp lookout, Bucky," Nolan commanded. "Now, let's go back to the way things usually are. Remember, Marshal, you can still get through this in one piece."

"Liar," Marty grumbled.

"Watch your tongue, boy!" Nolan shouted, drawing out his knife. "Remember what I said."

Ev gripped Marty's hand and led him toward the stable. Susan brought what was left of the coffee out and filled cups.

"Got to give you this, Marshal," young Ben said when his uncle left to visit the privy. "You do have an eye for the lookers. I wouldn't mind curlin' up with this one on a cold winter's eve."

Buck laughed loudly from his perch on the stable roof.

"I can't stand this," Marty whispered to his father. "We're so helpless."

"We'll have our chance, son," Ev said, gritting his teeth as Ben danced around Susan, pulling at the folds in her skirt, humming ditties and running the palm of his hand against her waist. "Stop it!" Ev shouted.

"Marshal ain't goin' to bother anybody," Stacy said, swinging his rifle in Ev's direction. Marty slipped away toward the little ones. Rachel wrapped herself around Finley's skinny legs. Todd covered his ears.

"Well, little lady, can't we have a dance?" Ben asked, bowing mockingly.

Susan drew back, glanced around for some sign of Nolan, then removed the lid from the coffee pot. Before Ben had a chance to react, she threw the remaining liquid at the young outlaw's face. The scalding coffee flew into Ben's eyes, burned his forehead and cheeks. Ben screamed, clutched his face, and stumbled toward the water trough.

"Ahhh!" Ben yelled. "Bucky?"

Buck slid down the roof and rushed to his brother's side. Nolan cursed loudly from the privy back of the house. Ev started for Susan, but Lou Stacy blocked the way. Ev caught a glimpse of Hazlewood as Marty waved toward the water hole. Finley dragged Rachel along. Todd grabbed the water bucket and scrambled after them.

Lord, go with them, Ev prayed as the youngsters made their escape. Only Marty remained, standing stiffly between Rip Hazlewood and the others.

Minutes later Nolan emerged from the privy, hurriedly fastening his pants and buckling on his gunbelt.

"What's happened?" Nolan shouted.

"She threw coffee in Ben's face!" Buck announced. "Burned him somethin' awful!"

Nolan glanced around the buildings, noticed Stacy was watching Ev, Hazlewood had Marty, then stepped back ashen-faced.

"Rip, did you lock up the little ones?" Nolan asked.

"Aren't they here?" Hazlewood gasped.

"They've gone!" Stacy said, kicking a rock halfway across to the stable. "Ben, this is your doin', messin' with her like that!"

"You were doin' what?" Nolan growled, stomping toward the two Wood boys. "What'd you do, Ben, wait till I was away till you had your fun? Well, I'll show you what's fun!"

Nolan swung a big fist and laid young Ben out on the porch.

"And you, Bucky!" Nolan yelled, grabbing Buck by the shirt and flinging him to the ground. "You're supposed to be keepin' watch!"

"Ben was hurt," Buck explained, backing away from his angry uncle. "He was callin' for me."

"It's her fault," Ben declared, pointing up at Susan.

"Her fault?" Nolan shouted. "I suppose she made you do it, huh?"

Nolan kicked at Ben, sending the young man crawling off to safety.

"We've got to get them back," Stacy said, gazing over the barrel of his rifle at Ev. "Where'll they be, Marshal?"

"Halfway to the neighbors by now," Ev said, smiling.

Nolan charged forward, ignored Ev and slammed Martin hard against the storeroom wall.

"Where've they gone, boy?" Nolan thundered. "Where would they hide? You know. Tell me!"

"I'll tell you nothin'," Martin said, spitting at Nolan's face.

"Why you little. . ." Nolan shouted. But Rip Hazlewood stilled his uncle's hand.

"They can't be far," Hazlewood said. "Nearest neighbor's miles off. We've got the horses. Shoot, two of 'em's just little kids, Uncle George. Buck and I'll round 'em up."

Buck got to his feet and joined Hazlewood.

"Sure, Uncle George, we'll find 'em," Buck promised.

"Do it quick," Nolan ordered. "Or get on back. Don't forget the purpose at hand. That stage'll be here 'fore long."

Hazlewood nodded and led the way to the corral. In a flash, he and Buck had saddled two ponies and were headed after the fleeing children.

"Oh, Ev," Susan said, clutching Ev's arm as the outlaws headed out.

"Don't worry," Ev assured her. "Fin knows what to do. They'll be fine."

"And what about you?" she asked as Stacy unlocked the storeroom and pointed them inside. "Thank God Marty's still here. If they'd all gotten away. . ."

"What?" Ev asked as the door closed, leaving him and Susan, Martin, and Art alone in the darkness.

"I know you. If we were safe, you'd go after Nolan single-handed."

"But you're not all safe," Ev said, turning Martin's face toward him. "Why aren't you, Marty? I told you to go, too."

"You saw Rip," Marty said. "He might've followed us."

"You're fortunate he didn't shoot you," Ev said.

"Not after Tim," Marty said confidently. "I think I know him a little now."

"Don't count on that too much," Susan said. "I doubt he'd choose you over his uncle."

"Don't forget," Ev said somberly. "When it comes down to it, he'll hang as high as the others."

"I couldn't go, Pa," Marty said, slipping one arm around his mother and the other around Ev. "I'm not a boy anymore. I couldn't run out on you."

I know, Ev thought, shuddering. But I wish you could have, son. How I wish you could have!

CHAPTER 12

EV sat beside the door of the storeroom and stared through the cracks in hopes of glimpsing what was happening. It wasn't possible. He caught sight of Ben Wood bathing his face in springwater. Later he saw Lou Stacy on the porch, cradling his Winchester and keeping watch on the road from whence the westbound stage would appear. Hazlewood and Buck were out searching the countryside for the children, of course. George Nolan had seemingly disappeared.

"What do you see?" Susan asked, leaning against his shoulder.

"Nothin'," he told her. "Less than nothin'. I can't even see Nolan. We're worse off than ever. At least before I knew where they were."

"If only the stage'd get here," Martin said, stepping to the door and peering through the cracks. "Why can't it come now, when there's just three of 'em?"

"Can't ask for too awful much," Ev said, pulling Martin down beside him. "If it hadn't been late, we might never've got anybody away."

"Guess you're right," Marty reluctantly agreed. "Still. . ."

"I know," Ev said, turning Martin over to his mother, then crawling across to where Art Hyland lay. "Art, can you hear me?"

"I hear you," Art grumbled, rolling over on his uninjured side. "Think I was dead, Ev?"

"Probably ought to be," Ev said, cheering at the sound of the driver's voice. "Feel like some food?"

"Not just now," Art said, fighting to sit up. "Bet you never thought you'd hear that from me?"

"Not where Susan's cookin' was concerned," Ev said. "You know they shot young Tim Merritt."

"Oh?" Art asked. "That's a pure shame. I liked that boy. He used to ride out and meet the coach on past the breaks sometimes. Every once in a while he'd climb up and ride shotgun a mile or two. Yeah, I liked that boy."

"He was my friend," Martin said, his voice trembling. "We used to go after deer when there weren't too many chores waitin'. Tim wasn't much of a shot, though. Skinnier'n Fin, just bones with a little flesh added on so he wouldn't spook folks. Remember when he'd jump in the water hole? You'd think somebody'd thrown a stick in."

"I remember the way he'd beg for a biscuit," Susan whispered. "I'd always give him one, but some days I'd wait till he got down on both knees."

"You used to make him sing," Ev remembered. "Poor Tim wasn't much for carryin' a tune, but he tried."

"And now he's dead," Marty snapped. "Why? 'Cause I had to let the horses go."

"We talked about that already," Ev reminded the boy. "It wasn't your doin'."

"No," Susan agreed. "It was this country, this wild, rolling wasteland, with hills here and there, a few trees around a spring. Is it worth fighting for, Ev? Worth dying for?"

"It's home," Ev told her. "I never thought it would be, you know."

"You wanted to stay in Jacksboro," Marty said.

"I lived most of my life along the Trinity," Ev told them. "But it's been good here. You called this a wasteland, Susan. It's not. The land gives life, if a man knows where to look. The springs water your garden, provide for the stock, give us what we need for ourselves and our guests. There may not be trees like in the East, but the ones here gave us lumber for repairin' the house, rebuildin' the stable, puttin' up the storeroom and the corral. We have plenty of firewood."

"And until now, we've been safe," Susan said. "Two years."

"They were good years, weren't they?" Ev asked.

"An illusion," Susan said tearfully. "What was it you used to call it, an oasis? Eden? I don't know, Ev. Maybe I expected too much. All I know for sure is I'm sitting here with my husband and my son. Out there a little boy lies dead. Rachel, my little baby, is off with Todd and Finley. . . maybe dead by now. And what about us?"

"We're next," Marty whispered.

"I don't know about that," Art objected. "You got the young ones out, did you?"

"Yes," Ev said, holding Susan tightly as she began to cry.

"Don't you see?" Art asked. "That changes everything."

"How?" Marty asked.

"Nolan can't kill us all, so he won't need to shoot anybody," Art said, wincing as pain from his shoulder raced up his neck.

"Is he right, Pa?" Marty asked hopefully. "Won't they just leave us locked up here when they finish?"

Ev glanced again outside. He couldn't even see Stacy now. The whole station appeared deserted.

"Ev?" Susan asked.

"Art's right," Ev explained. "There's no need of shootin' us all now."

"But that doesn't mean Nolan won't do it anyway," Marty objected. "Pa, I know Rip Hazlewood won't. Lou Stacy, either. If you can't shoot 'em all, at least get Nolan!"

"What?" Susan asked. "Shoot them? He doesn't even have a gun."

"Yes, I do," Ev said, calming Susan with a firm embrace. "Marty hid one in the stable."

"You've got to forget about it," she said, angrily pulling him away. "Art said it. They've got no reason to harm us now."

"Since when does George Nolan need an excuse?" Ev asked. "I know you don't want to hear this, Susan, but you have to. The kind of man Nolan is will never walk away from here without what he set out for. We've spoiled his plan. He'll have to take out his anger on someone."

"Who?" Susan asked nervously.

"Me, more than likely," Ev told her. "But it could be he'll want more blood."

"That's why you wanted me to go, isn't it?" Marty asked. Ev nodded, and Susan sobbed. "He might get us all anyway," Marty said. "There won't be anybody left to take care of Rachel and Todd. Fin's barely twelve."

"The Merritts will take them in," Susan said, lifting her head and drying her tears. "I know Sarah. She'll need someone to look after with Tim gone. Oh, Lord, I hope they're all right."

The discussion closed as the sound of approaching horses filled the air. Ev could see Hazlewood and Buck Wood dismount, then rush into the house. Nolan reappeared moments later. Together with Lou Stacy, they headed for the storeroom.

"They must not've found 'em," Ev said, pulling Martin away from the door. "No matter what they do, son, don't tell."

"I won't," Martin promised as a key turned in the lock. The door sprang open, and Nolan charged inside.

"Where are those kids?" Nolan roared. "Tell me!"

"Most likely already at the Merritts," Ev said. "Bill Merritt's probably collectin' his riders this very moment. You'd better clear out."

"No chance," Hazlewood said. "We spotted the boy's horse, traced the tracks. Anyone headed that way would've left a trail. They're someplace closer, likely holed up. You

got a hidin' place around here, don't you, Marty? Maybe
one even your pa doesn't know about?"

"You're crazy," Martin barked. "I told Fin to head for
the Merritt place."

"He could be tellin' the truth," Buck said. "They
could've stayed to the rocks. There's ground up there a
horse can't cross."

"Rip?" Nolan asked.

"Could you walk six, seven miles if you were a wisp of
a girl?" Hazlewood asked. "Neither of the boys is apt to
carry her. They've got to be holed up."

"Well, then we'd best find out where," Nolan said,
grabbing Martin's hand and dragging the boy outside.

"Help him, Ev," Susan pleaded. "Tell them."

"I don't know," Ev lied. "Neither does Martin."

"Thought marshals told the truth," Buck jeered. "No
bunch of rabbits finds a hole without somebody knowin'
it's there."

Hazlewood and Buck hauled Martin out of sight, and
Ev rushed toward the door. Stacy blocked the way. As
Marty cried out, Nolan glared through the open door.

"Now, what's come of that stage?" Nolan asked, kicking
the wall of the storeroom with a fury that rattled the roof.
"You supposed to post some signal? You warn 'em somehow?"

"Told you before," Art said, rolling back onto his back.
"There've been rains back East. Crossin' could be flooded.
Must be the rains."

"Rains my eye!" Nolan grumbled.

"It's a poor risk waitin' here any longer," Stacy said.
"Any moment a posse could ride in. Even if those kids
don't get to somebody, there's the stage. That kid on his
horse isn't the only one likely to stumble onto it. Stage late!
Might not come this week at all. Schedule's been off like
that before, dozens of times."

"You mean we could wait another week?" Nolan asked.

"Easy," Ev said. "I've known it delayed ten days, two weeks."

Nolan shook his head and walked back outside. Hazlewood dragged Marty from behind the stable, his shirt torn away from his chest. Blood trickled from the boy's lip. A bruise appeared on his left temple.

"Marty?" Susan called.

"He didn't say anything," Hazlewood grumbled. "I don't think he will, even if he knows."

"We didn't work on him much," Buck said, kicking the dirt. "I could use my knife, Uncle George."

"How 'bout that, Marshal?" Nolan asked. "Want Buck to get out his knife?"

"You'd be smarter to consider this," Ev said, brushing Stacy aside and walking past the door. "If that stage does come, I'll need help with the horses. They see strangers, they're apt to stand off till they get an explanation. Even now they'll see Marty's beaten some."

"He's right," Hazlewood said.

"I say shoot 'em, clear on out," Stacy said. "Could be the stage has been warned. Maybe they sent out a scout last night. Could be a dozen things wrong."

"It's the rains!" Art shouted. "Just the rains!"

"They've been late before," Marty managed to say as he limped toward his father. "We warned nobody."

"I say pull out, Uncle George," Ben called from the porch. "We've already been here too long."

"Too long to ride away with forty dollars and some horses," Nolan told them. "Twenty-five thousand's what the clerk said was ridin' on that coach. You ever seen that much money in your life? It's worth an extra risk or two."

"Or three," Buck added.

"Get yourselves back in that storeroom for now," Nolan said, grabbing Martin by the shoulder and tossing the battered boy inside. Ev dodged a fist and retreated on his own.

"You got off lucky," Hazlewood said as he closed the door. "Next time somebody's goin' to die, Marty."

"I hope it's you," Martin said angrily.

Hazlewood marched away, and Susan dipped a rag in the water bucket. Only now, in the dim light, could the whitish-pink marks left by a strap be detected on the leathery skin of Martin's back.

"I'll see him dead for that," Ev declared.

"I'm all right, Pa," Martin said, his face screwed up with pain as his mother tended the wounds. "I didn't tell them. It wasn't so bad."

"Worse'n that lickin' I gave you when you put manure in the school stove in Jacksboro?" Ev asked.

"Close," Martin said, trying to smile.

"I'll see if I can find some brine," Ev said, walking to the back of the room. "It does wonders for scrapes. My pa used it after a lickin'."

Ev rummaged through the stores. He finally found a bottle of horse liniment, and Susan used it instead.

"Still got that food about?" Art asked. "I guess maybe I could eat a little somethin' now."

"I'll get it," Martin volunteered, pulling out the slices of ham and bread Susan had saved for Art. "It's fair eatin'."

"I'll share it," Art offered. "Doesn't seem likely we'll get invited to dinner tonight."

"No," Ev agreed. "Not unless the stage arrives."

CHAPTER 13

THE stage didn't arrive, though. As the sun started its gradual descent into the western hills, Rip Hazlewood opened the door and ordered Ev, Susan, and Martin outside.

"I suppose you can stay in there," Hazlewood told Art.

"And us?" Ev asked.

"Uncle George sent for you," Hazlewood explained, pointing toward the house. Ev noticed the young outlaw held a tighter grip on his rifle than before. Lou Stacy watched from the stable, too. Nolan was clearly taking no more chances with his captives.

Hazlewood led the way through the kitchen and on into the dining room. Susan gasped as she looked upon a scene of utter disarray. The stove had been torn from the wall. Kettles and pots had been thrown through the windows. Shelves lay splintered about the floor, and even the tin plates had been slammed against the walls until they were barely recognizable.

"You'll be wanting those things when it's time for breakfast," Susan told Nolan.

"No, we won't," Nolan said, stuffing a slice of beef into his mouth. "You've cooked your last meal, ma'am."

Ev shuddered, not so much from the words themselves as from the tone of Nolan's voice, the deadly stare of those cold, dark eyes.

"What do you want from us?" Ev asked, stepping in front of Susan. "You didn't bring us here to share supper."

"No, we decided to have our meal in peace tonight," Nolan said, sharing a private laugh with Hazlewood and the Woods. "Thought a little hunger might put you in mind of those kids of yours, all alone out there, listenin' to wolves and such."

"We don't need to be reminded of them," Susan retorted.

"Oh, I think you do," Nolan continued. "I thought to bring 'em back, but after talkin' it over, we decided it'd be easier to leave 'em where they are. Less trouble in the mornin'. But as to the stage, I will have my answer. What have you done to warn it, Marshal? I talked to Lou. It's never this late."

"It is," Martin objected.

"Shut him up," Nolan said, motioning for Buck to keep Martin quiet. Buck pulled the boy over against the wall and whispered something. Martin turned slightly pale. He spoke nothing more.

"Art thinks it's the rains back East," Ev said. "We've got no signal save firin' off shots to warn a coach of trouble. You can send riders out. They'll tell you nothin's been up the road since you came in."

"It didn't come early, did it, Rip?" Nolan asked.

"No," Hazlewood said. "I would've seen it, Uncle George. No, it's just late."

"I won't wait much longer!" Stacy hollered from the front door. "It's dangerous stayin' here this long. Someone's bound to investigate. There's that boy, too."

"We should've buried him," Ben said. "Smell's gettin' bad."

"Take him off down the hill," Nolan instructed. "Lay him under some brush. Wolves'll do the rest."

"You can't!" Martin objected. Buck Wood knocked the boy to the floor.

"It wouldn't take long to bury him," Ev said. "Just a

shallow grave so his father can take him home later."

"Leave him to the wolves," Nolan said. "If I was you, I'd worry about myself."

"You're no better than an animal," Susan cried. "Smashing up everything out of pure meanness. Shooting that poor boy. Now leaving him out there for the animals. Can't you at least cover him up?"

"I could do a lot of things," Nolan said, "but I do what I have a mind to. That includes shootin' people. You, lady, are gettin' to be a regular boil on my behind, and I generally have those lanced."

Ev pulled Susan away and implored her to be silent.

"The stage'll be here tomorrow, and we'll pull out," Hazlewood said.

"Maybe it's time we moved along, stage or no stage," Ben said, gazing at his uncle. "This waitin' was never part of the plan, Uncle George."

"Plans change," Nolan declared. "It wasn't in my mind to stay this long, but who knew the stage'd be so late."

"Doesn't matter," Buck said. "Ben and I talked it over. We'll be movin' on."

"Rip?" Nolan asked.

"Me, too," Hazlewood told his uncle. "We've spent too much time here already. You know why we're successful, Uncle George. We hit fast and get away before anybody knows what's happened. Not even twenty-five thousand's worth stretchin' a rope for."

"If I had some boys with a little backbone. . ." Nolan grumbled.

"We've got backbone," Hazlewood complained. "We just don't take to shootin' kids, then hangin' around so their folks can come after us. Odds aren't with us, Uncle George."

"I know you hate to pull away from a thing," Ben said, "but sometimes you've got to pass up a flooded crossin' in order to get across a river. Waitin' just don't figure."

"We waited for that bank in Gainesville," Nolan reminded them. "Remember that?"

"Yeah, but we weren't holed up in the vault," Buck said. "We ended up shootin' women and a boy that time. Had half the countryside after us. Why, we spent six months in the Nations. Even then we had to ride into Kansas. That's no place for a Southern boy, Uncle George. We lost cousin Henry, old Corley up there, too. Henry, why, they shot him at the supper table, gave him no chance at all."

"And you still rode with him?" Ev asked, turning to Hazlewood.

"What else could I do?" Hazlewood asked, holding his hands out palm up. "Who'd give me a job? Only skill I know's handlin' a gun. Tell me, Marshal, would you hire me?"

"We treated you square," Marty reminded Hazlewood.

"Enough!" Nolan yelled. "I brought you here to answer some questions, not start a feud."

"So go ahead, ask me," Ev said. "Nothin' to keep you from it, is there?"

"Nothin' at all," Nolan said, grinning. "Actually, I don't know that I've got a lot to ask you, Marshal. Main thing is I want you to know what's to happen. Crack of dawn tomorrow, you and your boy there'll be out, tendin' to your chores. Mrs. Raymond there," Nolan added, pointing to Susan, "will be in the house with Lou. Anything happens. . . twig snaps, whatever. . . and that stage gets warned, she's the first to die. Understand?"

"I understand."

"Ben'll be just back of you in the stable door. Buck on the roof so he sees everything. Rip'll be watchin' your boy. And me, I'll be sittin' right beside the window, holdin' my sights on *you*."

Nolan laughed wickedly, and Susan leaned on Ev's arm. The outlaw leader then motioned to Hazlewood.

"Let's go along back to the storeroom now, Marshal,"

Hazlewood said. "Let's have an easy night of it, hear?"

Ev nodded as he led Susan and Martin from the house. Once they were safely locked away in the storeroom again, Ev filled in Art Hyland.

"Ever hear about a Judas goat, Ev?" Art asked.

"That the one that leads the sheep to the slaughter?" Ev replied. "Yeah, I get the point. That's us, leadin' the westbound on in so they can be shot, too."

"In the end they're bound to kill us all," Marty said, stretching out on the damp floor.

"They'll leave if the stage doesn't come soon," Ev said. "I hope for his sake Tom Shipley's late."

"Won't do us much good, though," Art muttered. "I'd hate to see Nolan really mad."

"I know," Ev agreed. "If the stage comes along, we might have a moment to scatter."

Ev then turned toward Susan. Her face was pale in the faint light. He pictured Lou Stacy standing beside her with a rifle. No, as long as she was in the house, how could anything be done?

"Any of that ham still around?" Marty asked. "I'm starvin'."

"A bit of it," Art said, passing over the last of the food.

"Ma, Pa?" Marty asked, offering to share.

Ev shook his head, and Susan declined as well.

"I wonder if the children are hungry?" Susan asked as she prepared her bed.

"I pray they're safe," Ev said. He gripped her hand.

"Will we be?" she asked.

"I don't know," Ev said, listening to the familiar chirping of the crickets down by the water hole. That sound, more than any other, took him back to the little farm where he'd grown up. It seemed all that belonged to another lifetime now.

He found other memories flooding his head. There was the night Martin was born amidst a spring thunderstorm, crashing thunder and brilliant flashes of lightning seemingly tearing the sky apart. The war had been over barely a year, and the noise took Ev back to the fighting, to the Yank gunners at Johnsonville, to a dozen campaigns he'd ridden with Bedford Forrest. It'd been a fierce night, but out of it had come Martin, the dark-haired son who'd filled the house with laughter, who'd splash away half the summer and fend off the despair of Texas winters.

Ev turned and stared through the cracks at the clear sky overhead. It was hard to see more than a few stars at a time, but he knew they were all up there, shining brightly as always. Yes, the world had a way of going on in spite of itself.

He frowned as he imagined little Tim Merritt thrown onto the hillside, his lifeless eyes shut off forever from those stars. As Ev envisioned the corpse, it suddenly changed. Instead there was Martin, was Susan, was Everett Raymond himself.

Ev blinked away the vision. He returned to the stark solitude of the storeroom. Art Hyland snored noisily five feet or so away. Martin rolled back and forth, thrashing his arms out against some invisible enemy. There he was, a terrified boy fighting hard to be a man. There should have been more time, Marty, Ev thought. I wanted to teach you so much, help you take those first steps toward manhood, catch you if you fell. But there was no time. There never was!

Ev slipped off his boots, pulled his shirttail out of his trousers and rested back on the hard ground beside Susan. She, too, was sleeping, silently, calmly, in spite of what Ev knew to be terrifying doubts.

As he closed his eyes, he found himself dreaming of the little ones. Fin would have a fire built. Todd and Rachel would huddle around their brother, asking a thousand questions little Finley couldn't answer. He would ration the food, keeping back some of it for the days ahead. Todd would grumble about that. The little boy was always hungry.

He'll worry about the chickens, Ev thought as he opened his eyes and tried to sweep away a rare tear. Todd and those accursed chickens. No one else could approach the hens without getting pecked half to death, but Todd would just whisper to them, pet the roosters, or bribe them with a bread crumb or two. Todd and his chickens!

Ev listened to the crickets again. He missed little Rachel most of all. She should be there, giving him a good night kiss, saying her prayers for Susan, playing some prank on Martin or Finley.

And Finley. . . Ev couldn't forget the thin boy's shivering shoulders, how frightened those little eyes had appeared when Tim Merritt was shot. It wasn't easy being Finley, the second son. Martin would always be oldest, most like their father. Todd would always be the little one, his mistakes forgiven, his pranks overlooked. Poor Fin, Ev thought, wishing he'd held the boy tighter that morning. I wonder if he knows I love him, too.

A second tear appeared in Ev's eye, wove its way across his cheek, dribbled over his chin, and dropped to his chest.

"I can't sleep much either," Susan whispered. "I can't get them out of my mind."

"Me, neither," Ev told her.

"At least it's not winter," she said. "They'll be warm enough. Todd catches a chill so easily."

"Yes, they're warm," Ev agreed.

"I should've put more food away for them. They shouldn't be hungry, not with all the smoked meats and tins of beans we've got at this place! I should have. . ."

"They couldn't carry much," Ev reminded her. "They'll be fine. You heard Nolan's men. They won't stay past tomorrow. We'll go bring them home then."

"Will we?"

"I won't consider anything else. You heard Art. It doesn't make sense to shoot us now."

"I heard Art, but I saw the look in Nolan's eyes, too. Stage or no stage, he's going to go after you. Tomorrow it will be over, you say? How, Ev? What will you do?"

"What I've always done," Ev said grimly. "Protect my family."

"How? You don't even know if that pistol is still hidden. What if Nolan's found it, unloaded the chambers?"

"I'll do whatever I can," he promised. "I'll try to see you and Marty aren't hurt."

"I know you'll try," she said, gazing off into the darkness. "Oh, Ev, I can't help worrying about the children. Who's going to make Rachel's dresses? Who'll mend Todd's torn britches, clip his hair? Who'll stay after Finley, see he does his lessons? Who will tell Martin how to sit with his first girl, teach him manners and how to keep the station accounts? There's so much left to show them, Ev. Who will. . ."

"We will," Ev told her. "You and I."

"I wonder if we'll ever see them again?" she asked, wrapping both arms around his chest and hugging him tightly. "Oh, Ev."

He felt her tears drop onto his cheek. He recognized the trembling fingers, the shallow breathing. Susan had been that way before, the cold spring morning in '62 when he'd ridden off to war, the moonless nights when he'd set off from Jacksboro in search of some lawbreaker.

"Don't forget, Susan," he told her. "I always come back."

"Yes," she said, hugging him even tighter. Through both their minds raced the same thought. But what about this time? Tim Merritt had expected to ride home that night, to lie in his bed dreaming of adventures. It takes such a short time, a second, really, to erase a dream, to silence a heartbeat.

"Oh, Ev," Susan cried a final time.

"I'm here, honey," he said. "I'll always be here."

But as they lay back on the ground and fought to catch a bit of sleep, he knew it was a promise that might not be kept. No, life came with few certainties. Life had always been so terribly temporary, so very temporary.

CHAPTER 14

EV awoke to the sound of a rooster crowing. It had been a long time since he'd slept so late. He eased Susan's head off his shoulder, then pulled on his boots.

"Think they'll really leave if the stage doesn't come to-day?" Marty asked, crawling over from the door. "Pa?"

"I don't know, son," Ev said, smoothing out a rebellious strand of his son's hair. "Nolan never agreed to that, and things bein' as they are, I can't see Lou Stacy or Hazlewood or those two brothers decidin' anything for themselves."

"Stage'll probably come anyway," Marty said.

Ev nodded, then gently nudged Susan to life.

"Is it morning already?" she asked, rising slowly. "Seems like we just went to sleep."

"I know," Ev agreed. "Best get dressed. They'll be over here before long."

Susan flashed a smile at Ev, patted Marty on the arm, and busied herself dressing. When she finished, she sat on the floor, staring around at the empty floor where Rachel, Todd, and Finley might have been.

"They're all right," Martin told her. "Off in that cave. I'll bet Fin's turned it into an adventure. He's one for the stories, Ma! He'd keep me up half the night with one of his tales."

"I remember how he used to come into the jailhouse," Ev said, smiling as the memory flooded his mind. "He'd pick up one of the posters from my desk. Next thing you knew, he'd have a whole story made up about the man."

"I remember those stories," Susan said. Her face

brightened as she reflected on Fin. But her smile faded as reality seeped in.

"Try not to think about them," Ev suggested. "It can't be too much longer, Susan. Just keep yourself busy."

"Doing what?" she asked as the morning's first tear trickled down her cheek.

"Whatever's handy," Ev said, picking up a fallen tin of beans and returning it to its shelf. "We can move the flour barrels around."

"Not much point to that," Martin said.

"Just keepin' busy," Ev explained.

Art Hyland awoke then, and Ev motioned Martin toward the shelves. Susan came over, and Ev helped her examine Art's shoulder.

"Seems to be drainin' well enough," Ev observed.

"I'll change the dressing tomorrow," Susan said.

"Tomorrow?" Art asked. "Figure we'll still be here?"

"In this storeroom?" Ev asked. "Not likely." He moved over to where Marty was organizing the tins on one shelf.

"Pa, you think maybe we could break one of these open?" Marty asked. "I'm awful hungry."

"Beans for breakfast?" Ev asked. "I never much cared for tins of beans anytime."

"There are all sorts of things over there," Susan said, leaving her patient long enough to point out where everything was. "The peaches were fine. How about some more?"

"We usually get half a man's wages for peaches in the summer," Marty grumbled. "But right now. . ."

"Open 'em up," Ev said. "I'm hungry myself."

"How do you tell what's what?" Marty asked, lifting three tins. Each was the same shape and size.

"Read the label," Susan told the boy.

"How?" Marty asked, tossing one tin to Ev. "You can't read anything in this light."

Ev held the tin near the door where the morning sun seeped through the cracks.

"Beans," Ev said, tossing it back.

"Try this one," Marty said, throwing a second tin over. After a few more tries, they were able to find several tins of peaches, two of apricots, and some beef hash.

"Shame we don't have a fire," Ev said, using Susan's smuggled kitchen knife to gash the side of each tin. "We could have a regular feast."

"Cold hash isn't my notion of a feast," Art complained.

But in truth the cold hash and tinned fruit brought them back to life. By the time Rip Hazlewood opened the door, Ev was growing hopeful. Any moment Bill Merritt might appear. Maybe the stage wouldn't come. Maybe, as Art had suggested, Nolan would ride away, leaving behind only a bitter memory and the corpses of the gambler and young Tim Merritt.

"Uncle George says it's time you were at your chores," Hazlewood announced. "Stage could be here soon."

"Not for a while," Martin said, gazing at the rising sun. "If they spent the night at the Brazos crossings, it'll be a good hour yet. Shame Pa doesn't still have his watch."

"It's half past seven," Hazlewood announced, dangling the watch from its chain.

"That belongs to my pa," Martin said angrily. "You're a lowdown thief."

"Never professed to be anything else, Marty," Hazlewood said. "Course, I was considerin' leavin' this behind when I ride off. If I hadn't taken it, Buck would have."

"I suppose," Martin admitted. "You could've hidden it someplace."

"Where? I don't have your talent for hidin' things. Or people," Hazlewood added.

Ev tensed. Had Hazlewood found the children? Did he know about the cave?

"I'd better see about feeding the chickens," Ev said, breaking the tension.

"Todd always leaves the feed in the corner of the stable, Pa," Martin explained, following his father from the storeroom.

"You, Mrs. Raymond, are expected in the kitchen," Hazlewood told Susan. "Seems Uncle George decided to have himself some breakfast after all."

"He'll have to eat it on his lap," Susan bristled. "He destroyed the plates."

"Oh, he found some wooden bowls." Ben said, stepping over to conduct Susan to the house. "Figured you could fix some eggs."

As Ev returned from the stable with the feed sack, he was surprised to find Susan coaxing an egg from a nervous hen.

"Let me," he offered, sprinkling grain across the coop, then collecting the eggs from under the reluctant hens.

"You do that almost as well as Todd does," Susan said. she laughed as a rooster took a nip at Ev's leg. "He may find himself out of a job."

"He can have it back soon as he returns," Ev assured her. "I saw all the chickens I ever wanted to see when I was ten."

Ev collected the eggs in his hands, then passed them along to Susan. As she retired to the kitchen, he continued feeding the birds, whistling one of Todd's tunes to keep them from stirring about.

"I thought for a minute Todd was back," Martin said, joining his father. "What should I do, Pa?"

"Look over the horses. I hate leavin' them in that corral all this time with no exercise. You did give 'em a run th' other day, but it's not like regular exercise. I hope those animals don't end up carryin' Tom Shipley's coach to Albany. Poor grays might just break down."

"It's Tom's fault for bein' late," Marty said.

"Him bein' late likely saved your brothers and sister," Ev reminded the boy. "Could be the salvation of us all."

"I don't think so," Marty said, gazing intently at the woodpile. "I know they're gettin' restless, but you're right. Nolan calls the tune. Th' others just dance along."

But that morning they weren't dancing very harmoniously. No sooner had Susan pulled a skillet full of bacon off the stove than Lou Stacy began shouting.

"I told you, George!" Stacy yelled. "I'm not sayin' it again. Someone's bound to come lookin' for that boy! We've got to get out while we still can."

"If they go pokin' around, lookin' for the boy, they're apt to find him," Nolan chortled. "Likely halfway gone to worms by now. Or wolves!"

"Stacy's right," Ben Wood spoke up. "Even if they don't find the eastbound stage, don't come across that boy, they're bound to wander by the station. Place like this just doesn't go half a week without company."

"This one does," Nolan argued. "It's why we picked it. No big ranches nearby. What travelers do come usually ride the stages. With both of 'em due the same day, we weren't likely to run into unexpected arrivals."

"Only thing is," Hazlewood said, "the next station may wonder why the eastbound hasn't gotten in. Stationmaster might hold up the westbound if he suspects trouble."

"I never thought of that," Nolan grumbled. "You could be right, Rip. Figure the marshal knew right along?"

"Don't know it myself for sure," Hazlewood said. "We could send a messenger to say the eastbound had itself an accident."

"Who'd you send, Stacy?" Nolan asked. "Why, they'd hardly believe him. The rest of us are postered. Some smart deputy happens along about the time you ride over there, he'll put the pieces together and have half the lawmen in the state out here."

"Seems a good argument for leavin'," Stacy declared. "They could be on their way already."

"No!" Nolan shouted. "We're goin' nowhere. It's not our way. We come. We stay till we get what we came after. Then we ride—not before!"

"Uncle George," Hazlewood pleaded, "you know as well as I do sooner or later that boy'll be missed. There's the little ones to think on, too. Somebody's bound to bring help. Any man rides out here's unlikely to pay such casual attention to us as that boy. It's not safe overstayin' our welcome. If that stage's comin' today, it ought to be in by midday. I'm for waitin' that long. If it's not here then, I say we should cut and run."

The others loudly voiced their agreement.

"So that's how you want it?" Nolan asked. "A fortune waitin' for us, and you'd just walk away, let it go?"

"My hide's worth somethin'," Stacy said.

"You didn't value it so high when you came to me after the stage line fired you," Nolan reminded Stacy. "Back then you begged to come along, said you'd do whatever I said."

"That was a long time ago," Stacy said. "I'm growin' nervous. The boys are, too. Would those three kids ever've gotten loose from us if we weren't all tired?"

"No," Nolan agreed. "So, you'll wait till noon, will you?"

"Till noon," Stacy said. The others mumbled their agreement.

"Then we'll pull out at noon if the stage isn't here before," Nolan said. "Which brings me to that other matter."

"We'll discuss that among ourselves," Hazlewood said.

It wasn't possible to hear the rest of the discussion. The voices of the outlaws calmed, and the wind stirred the leaves on the nearby trees. Ev knew what they were discussing, though. Who would live and who would die.

"The team's all ready for the stage," Martin called out from the corral.

"Fine, son," Ev said, waving Martin over.

"You got the pistol yet?" Martin whispered. "You're goin' to check to see it's loaded?"

"Would seem like the smart thing to do," Ev agreed. "Only I see Ben's watchin' us. Maybe later."

"I thought about lettin' the horses go again, Pa, but Buck's on the roof. I didn't see him, but the sun reflected off his rifle."

Ev scanned the roof. Sure enough, Buck's shadow fell across the cedar shingles.

"Don't know how wise it'd be to try anything," Ev cautioned. "Nolan's jumpy as is. He might start shootin' right away. Don't forget. Your ma's inside."

"I know."

"So I suppose all we can do is wait. And wait and wait and wait."

Martin nodded. The two of them then brought out the harness and began replacing one stretch of worn leather with a fresh piece. They'd only been working on it a few minutes when Rip Hazlewood appeared.

"We'll be leavin' soon," Hazlewood said, opening the watch and following the second hand as it made its way around the dial. "Guess nobody'll ever give me a watch like this one."

"They don't have to," Ev remarked. "You stole one."

"I'm not always particular proud of what I do, Marshal," Hazlewood said, closing the watch and gathering the chain. "But I don't apologize for myself. I never had much chance to be anything better. My folks died young, and th'only one around who didn't send me packin' was Uncle George."

"He did you a big favor," Ev said. "He taught you his trade."

"Not for a long time," Hazlewood explained. "He never asked a one of us to ride with him. My brother Henry, bein' the oldest, went first."

"He's the one you were talkin' about last night," Martin said. "The one that got shot at the supper table."

"In the back," Hazlewood snapped. "Right in front of me. Henry wasn't but a year older than I was. Well, when Uncle George went after the ones that shot Henry, I rode, too. Then later, when we got thinned out some, Ben and Buck came, too."

"They're learnin' fast," Ev noted. "Buck killed Tim easily enough."

"Wasn't always that way," Hazlewood said, fondly gazing a final time at the watch before passing it along to Martin. "I remember when he was like little Todd, runnin' around, feedin' the chickens and playin' the dickens with the pigs. When his ma took sick, he prayed every night. She died, though, and he took up shootin' things. First it was rabbits and squirrels. Later it was men."

"Tim wasn't a man," Martin complained. "He didn't even have a gun. Was no need to shoot him twice. Then to toss him out there like he was nothin'."

"None of this is how I intended it to be," Hazlewood confessed.

"Nor I," Ev said.

"I figured we'd be in and out of here before anybody knew what happened. All in one day, fast as wildfire."

"And now you know the truth, huh? One way or another, there'll be people buried here today. One man's already lyin' under the trees. There's a boy barely fourteen dead."

"And another standin' right here," Martin said, stretching himself to his full five feet four inches. "You mean to shoot me, too, Rip?"

"I didn't th' other day," Hazlewood reminded them. "But keep this in mind, Marshal, Marty. I'm not th'only one with a gun. When the shootin' starts, you best run like thunder. Uncle George won't hurt Mrs. Raymond."

"He shot women in Gainesville," Ev pointed out.

"They got in the way. Stacy's not one to set the law on his trail."

"And if the coach isn't here by noon?" Ev asked.

"Best pray it is, Marshal," Hazlewood said, glancing nervously toward the house. "If it isn't, prayers won't help a whole lot."

"Just me, or all three of us?" Ev asked.

Hazlewood didn't reply, just walked off toward the porch. Ev wasn't sure he wanted an answer anyway.

"Want your watch, Pa?" Martin asked, passing the watch toward Ev."

"Why don't you keep it for a while, son," Ev said. "You always were one for keepin' track of the timetables and such. I used to think that watch brought me luck. You keep it with you."

"You might need it more than me."

"Keep it all the same, Marty. Now, I wonder if we can find that pistol."

Martin lifted the harness so that it rested on the far end of the woodpile. As Ev moved along, checking the straps, he located the revolver. It wasn't difficult to check the cylinders. Each held a bullet.

"See you're keepin' busy, Marshal!" Nolan shouted from the house then.

"I'm doin' as I usually do," Ev told the outlaw. "That's what you told us, remember?"

"I remember," Nolan said, his eyes flashing dangerously.

"His eyes are so cold," Martin whispered. "I feel like ice's runnin' down my back."

"I know," Ev said, feeling those eyes boring through his back.

"Ever wonder what's behind those eyes?" Martin asked.

"I hope you never have to find out," Ev answered.

They then lifted the harness off the woodpile and carried it to the back of the stable. As they set it down, a howl came from the roof, sending splinters of terror through them both.

"Look, Uncle George!" Buck cried out.

Ev turned toward the road. A spiral of dust danced across the distant plain, creeping ever onward toward Calvary Hill. The westbound had come at last.

So, it's time, Ev thought, eyeing the pistol in the woodpile. It's time.

CHAPTER 15

GEORGE Nolan hadn't acquired a price on his head for nothing. Within seconds he was seemingly everywhere, issuing orders, locating his men, and attending to the captives. Lou Stacy crouched beside the front window of the house, holding his rifle on Ev and Martin. Susan was pinned at his side, shielding the former driver from fire.

Buck was safely hidden on the roof. Up there his rifle covered the stage's approach as well as the open ground between the stable, the house and the storeroom.

Ben concealed himself behind the corner of the house. He effectively cut off any escape route Ev might have conceived. Rip Hazlewood joined Ev in carrying the harness to the ready corral. Nolan himself made a rapid swing through the stable, then assured himself everything was normal elsewhere. He took only a moment to inspect the storeroom.

"Nearly forgot about this one," Nolan said, eyeing Art Hyland.

"He's nothin' to worry yourself over, Uncle George," Hazlewood said. "Won't do much good with a lame shoulder, and he's only awake half the time."

"Best gag him anyway," Nolan declared, waving Ben over. "He's got a tongue."

Ben trotted through the door, and Ev could hear Art groaning as the gag was applied. There were sounds of a brief struggle, but Ben reappeared shortly, motioning that the task had been completed.

"Now you remember what I said about your woman,"

Nolan told Ev, nodding toward the house. "Anything at all upsets my plan, she takes the first shot."

"I understand," Ev replied acidly.

"How about you, pup?" Nolan asked, turning to Martin.

"You just see she's not hurt," Martin said, glaring at the outlaw captain.

"Oh, he scares me," Nolan joked as he made his way back to the house. "You boys tremblin'?"

Ben laughed loudly, but Buck motioned for silence. The stage was close enough to be heard now, rumbling up the hill toward Antelope Springs. The tired horses struggled against the grade, knowing soon they'd have a rest. Soon they'd be able to taste the cool, clear water in the trough.

Ev glanced a final time around the station, *his* station. Yes, it was *his* place, *his* family. Who did Nolan think he was, riding in like this, tearing the family apart, threatening Susan and the children!

"Keep your mind on the purpose at hand," Nolan called from the doorway, swinging his Winchester first at Ev, then toward Martin.

"It'd be pure stupid to try anything now, Marshal," Rip Hazlewood whispered from a few feet away.

Ev turned and frowned. Hazlewood had abandoned his rifle, but he held a loaded Colt behind his back. That gun would deal death at the hint of an outcry, the first sound of a warning.

"Pa, what'll we do?" Martin asked as the stage closed the last fifty yards.

Ev eyed the pistol's hiding place, then glanced at Susan. What good would a shout do? They'd all be killed in a second. As to the stage, it stood little more chance than the eastbound. Nolan planned well. There was no denying it.

"Whoa!" young Tom Shipley cried, drawing the coach to a halt twenty yards or so short of the stable. "Whoa!"

Ev felt his legs give way. Why stop? Did Tom know about the Nolan gang? Or was it some new procedure?

"Nice mornin'," Tom called when the stage came to a stop.

"Was beginnin' to worry about you, Tom," Ev said, leaving the corral and stepping toward the coach. "You're late."

"We found ourselves held up on account of heavy rains. All the Brazos crossings were flooded. We had to wait for the water level to drop."

"Unusual to have so much rain in summer," Ev said, reading alarm in Tom's twenty-year-old eyes. For a young driver, Shipley was veteran cautious.

"Lots of strange things about," Shipley said, scanning the buildings for something out of the ordinary.

"Like you stoppin' short?" Ev asked.

Shipley turned to his guard, Joe Gilbert. Ev had known Gilbert close on twenty years now. They'd ridden together with the rangers. Gilbert wasn't much for saying anything, but he was a crack shot. Gilbert nodded to Shipley, and the young driver spoke again.

"Well, you know, Ev, we're carryin' a full load today. They had some trouble back in Ft. Worth. A pair of renegades tried to take the cashbox. Got themselves killed."

Before Ev could respond to the news, a tall, raw-boned man wearing a dusty hat leaned out the window and tapped the side of the coach.

"Driver, aren't we goin' on in?" the passenger asked. "My wife's quite weary."

"We'll be along shortly, Mr. Bunting," Shipley told the man.

"We're all tired," a second passenger spoke. "And I'm a day late already for Al Shepherd's wedding."

Ev spotted the familiar face of Parson Mills, the Baptist preacher from Albany. The preacher had set off three weeks back to visit a sick sister in Weatherford. There appeared to be one other passenger, a slender, bearded fellow sitting alongside the parson. Dan Baker, once an army scout, horse raiser, and most recently a buffalo hunter.

"I'd like to move us on through, Parson, but we have to be careful," Shipley explained. "If that agent sold the cash schedule once, he might've done it twice. You know that."

"Sold the schedule, did he?" Rip Hazlewood asked, laughing. "Hard to find reliable help nowadays, I suppose."

"Who's he?" Gilbert asked, warily swinging his rifle in Hazlewood's direction. "Never knew you to need outside help, Ev. Not with all those youngsters of yours."

"Ma. . . took the little ones. . . out to Waco," Martin stammered. "Just me and Pa here now. Rip was passin' through, and he agreed to stay and help a week or so."

"That right, Ev?" Shipley asked.

Ev nodded.

"There's been more trouble than high water," Gilbert said, keeping a sharp eye on Hazlewood. "We passed Tim Merritt's older brother a mile back. I promised we'd ask after young Tim. Seems he left home yesterday and hasn't come back. Said he was returnin' a horse to you."

"Seen him, Marty?" Shipley asked.

"Yes, sir," Marty said, stepping closer to his father. "He was by yesterday. But he rode on."

"Tom said he had that little mustang you're so proud of," Shipley continued, searching Marty's face for the truth. "You usually keep that horse in the ready corral, Marty. He's not there now."

"We, uh, put him in the stable," Ev broke in. "Has a sore foot."

"Didn't seem to bother him much when he ran past us an hour ago," Shipley said, tying the reins to the brake and dropping his hands slowly toward the floor. Most drivers kept a spare rifle hidden there.

"Must be another horse, mister," Hazlewood said, sliding in between Ev and Marty. "Lots of mustangs 'round here. Some look awful close to the same."

"Don't know your new hand here," Gilbert said. "What'd you say his name was, Marty?"

"Rip, Rip Hazlewood," the boy said nervously.

"You seem awful skittish, Ev," Shipley pointed out. "You sure everything's all right?"

"What'd be wrong?" Ev asked. "I know you're shook by that business back in Ft. Worth, but there's nothin' here to concern yourself with."

"You sure?" Shipley asked. "Word's out George Nolan's been through these parts. He's a bad one, Ev. You remember that job he pulled in Gainesville?"

Ev nodded. Each second passed like an hour now. He glanced at Susan's face in the window. Nolan inched forward, cautiously keeping to the shadows. Hazlewood was only inches from Ev's back.

"Haven't seen him, either," Ev told the driver.

"Well, Joe?" Shipley said, turning to the guard.

"Guess it's all right," Gilbert said.

Suddenly there was a woman's cry from the house. Lou Stacy crashed through the window onto the porch, bellowing as he grabbed his bleeding forehead. Susan had shoved him.

"Now, Bucky!" Nolan commanded.

In an instant the station became an inferno of gunfire. Ev knocked Hazlewood aside, grabbed Marty and pulled the boy through the door of the stabie only seconds before bullets tore apart the wall beside them.

The stable wasn't the only target. Buck had fired rapidly from the roof, and Joe Gilbert hung limply from the top of the stage. Tom Shipley had managed to crawl down unharmed and was now returning fire. Stacy and Nolan peppered the coach from the shelter of two barrels on the porch. Ben raced to the woodpile and joined in.

"If only we'd left the pistol inside," Marty grumbled as the outlaws' shots took effect. Parson Mills dragged a woman out the back of the coach toward the safety of a nearby oak. The load boom of a Sharps buffalo gun from behind the rear wheels told Ev that Dan Baker had joined the fray. There was no sign of the impatient Mr. Bunting, but Ev noticed there were several holes in the side of the coach. Likely one of Nolan's shots had found its target.

"You get clear in time, Ev?" Shipley called from the stage.

"Sure, Tom!" Ev answered.

"I knew somethin' was wrong when that boy disappeared. I sent Tom Merritt home to bring help."

Shipley had little time to talk further. While Buck kept Dan Baker pinned down, Nolan motioned for the others to advance. Rip Hazlewood raced along the side of the stable until he reached the safety of a clump of small trees. Nolan and Stacy rolled their barrels forward, shielding themselves from return fire. Ben sprang forward, too, but got only as far as the corner of the stable. The Sharps exploded again. Its heavy ball, intended for a charging buffalo, tore through Ben's chest and sent the young man spinning crazily to the ground.

"Ben!" Buck screamed from the roof. But Ben Wood never answered. Dan Baker had seen to that.

A fury of gunfire now enfiladed the stagecoach. Ev stared through the doorway, watching the three outlaws outside.

"I'm goin' after the pistol," Ev told Marty. "Keep clear, son."

Marty nodded, then crawled behind a saddle and huddled against the wall. Ev wanted to reach out, touch the boy's hand, leave him something to hold onto. But there wasn't any time. No one could hold the coach for long, not even Tom Shipley and an old buffalo hider. Ev leaped out the door, rolled alongside the woodpile and reached for the hidden Colt.

It wasn't there!

"Lookin' for this, Marshal?" Nolan jeered as he held up the missing gun. "Didn't think I knew about it, did you? Should've made your move earlier."

Ev hugged the ground as Nolan fired into the woodpile. He could hear Marty's groans from the stable, Susan's muffled cries from inside the house.

Get out of there, Susan, he silently implored her. Get out the back, run down to the cave. Nolan seemed to read Ev's thoughts.

"We'll tend to her shortly," Nolan assured him.

Ev shuddered. Glancing at the stage, he noticed Shipley's rate of fire had fallen off. Dan Baker had to reload his rifle after each shot. Hazlewood leaped forward, rushing to within ten feet of the stage before halting. Nolan charged from the house, firing rapidly. Stacy kept behind the barrels.

"Oh, God," Ev said as Nolan climbed up onto the roof of the coach. The firing grew worse than ever. Ev expected any second to hear Tom Shipley or Dan Baker scream out in death, but Nolan wasn't concerned with them. His attention was focused on the cashbox. As Dan Baker made a break for the trees, Shipley rolled away from the coach. Nolan released the brake and slapped the horses into motion.

"Yah!" Nolan screamed. The stage jolted into motion. Soon it was rumbling back toward the house. Rip Hazlewood raced over and climbed aboard. As it rolled past the house, Ev jumped to his feet and sped to where Ben Wood's discarded rifle rested in the dust. While the outlaws were occupied with stopping the lathered horses, Ev grabbed the Winchester, then pried a box of shells from Ben's lifeless hand.

As Ev drew back, the ground beside his right foot exploded. Ev glanced up in time to see Buck Wood raise his rifle for a second shot. But it was Ev who fired instead, hitting Buck solidly in the left hip.

"Uncle. . ." Buck called out. The young gunman dropped to one knee, then rolled screaming down the far side of the roof. Ev heard him drop from the eaves and land hard on the ground below. There wasn't time to make a more careful examination. Nolan stopped the coach, and Lou Stacy sent a shot in Ev's direction.

"Hold your fire a minute!" Nolan screamed as the horses reared and whined. Dan Baker resumed firing from the oaks, but Stacy took careful aim on the crouching buffalo hunter, then fired. Dan Baker fell.

"I told you to hold your fire!" Nolan screamed, lifting the metal cashbox and sending it crashing to the ground. "Do as you're told, Stacy!"

"I'll do what I have to!" Stacy snarled. "I aim to stay alive."

Rip Hazlewood stepped out of the stagecoach and slapped the horses back into motion. The coach roared on past the stable, affording Ev the chance to retreat.

"Come on, son," Ev said, filling the Winchester's magazine as he kept watch on the outlaws. "We're gettin' out of here."

"Where?" Marty asked, hovering beside his father.

"Out the back, then around the house," Ev explained. "Your ma's still in there. We'd best beat Nolan to her."

"What about Buck?" Martin asked, pointing to the roof.

"We'll see about him on the way," Ev said, grabbing the boy's arm and leading the way to the back door. Shots tore into the wall of the stable near the door, following Ev and Martin as they fled the stable. Ev hesitated at the back door, then swung it open and glanced quickly outside. Buck Wood lay in a heap ten feet away, his head nodding eerily toward the left.

"Pa?" Martin asked as Ev collected Buck's guns.

"Must've landed on his head," Ev explained as he hugged the wall of the stable. "Likely broke his neck."

Martin's face grew pale, but he took the rifle Ev passed into his hands. Ev stuffed the pistol under his belt.

"There are three of them left," Ev explained. "Nolan, Stacy, and Hazlewood. I don't know for sure, but I think some of the stage passengers are all right. If Tom's not shot, he'll help. We're going to try to keep Nolan's bunch between us and Tom."

Martin nodded his understanding, but as they tried to leave the shelter of the stable, Ev saw it was too late. Nolan and Hazlewood were headed for the corral, dragging the cashbox along between them. Stacy lurked behind, covering the withdrawal.

"Get down!" Ev shouted, pushing Martin's head toward the ground as a bullet tore through the air overhead.

"George!" Stacy yelled. "I'm almost out of shells. Toss me a box!"

"You won't need many," Nolan called out as he shot the lock from the cashbox.

"Nolan!" Stacy pleaded as he fired again in Ev's direction, then discarded his empty rifle.

Ev pointed toward the storeroom and opened fire on Nolan's retreating shadow. Martin charged across the open ground, but Stacy failed to fire. The former driver drew his pistol and opened up instead on a figure weaving its way through the cedars near the back of the stable.

"That you, Tom?" Ev asked as Martin fired his first shot from the storeroom.

"Yeah, Ev," Tom replied. "They're gettin' away with the payroll. Can you stop 'em?"

"Don't know," Ev said, flinching as two rifles barked from the corral. Neither seemed to be aiming at anyone in particular. Seconds later the gate opened, and a pair of horses emerged from the herd.

"Don't leave me!" Stacy pleaded, emerging from his hiding place as Hazlewood and Nolan mounted their ponies.

Tom Shipley reacted first, dropping Stacy to his knees.

"Two of 'em got clear!" Tom yelled to Ev.

Ev stared at the fleeing horsemen, then turned to Martin. The boy leaned against the storeroom, his face suddenly ashen. Ev then glanced at the porch where Lou Stacy crawled along, his hand still dragging the pistol.

"That's far enough, Stacy!" Ev yelled. "Drop the gun."

"Sure, Ev," Stacy said, coughing as he shook the pistol loose from limp fingers. "Doesn't much matter now."

"Where will they go?" Shipley demanded to know.

"Nowhere particular," Stacy said through a mouthful of blood.

"You didn't have a meeting place?" Ev asked. Stacy shook his head. "You sure?" Ev asked. "Nolan seemed awful careful about his plans."

"Didn't. . . didn't," Stacy said, choking.

"Didn't what?" Shipley asked, kneeling beside the wounded outlaw.

"Didn't. . . tell me," Stacy said, gazing up with moist eyes. "I'd tell. . . you. . . if I knew!"

Ev nodded. Stacy wasn't the sort to overlook a thing like Nolan's betrayal. But it was clearly no point to press. Stacy sprawled on the porch, his eyes fixed skyward.

"Ev?" Susan cried from behind the bolted door of the house.

"It's all right," Ev called to her, shaking off the terrible fatigue that permeated his entire being. "It's all over."

Susan cracked open the door, then raced to his side. As her arms held him tightly, Ev dropped the Winchester and leaned against her suddenly strong frame. Marty ran over, and the three of them sank into the soft ground beside the porch.

"Art Hyland's locked in the storeroom," Ev mumbled to Tom Shipley. "Let him out, will you?"

Ev then closed his eyes and allowed Susan and Marty to hold him erect. The blood and the dust and the terror had taken their toll.

CHAPTER 16

ONCE the smoke and dust began to settle, Ev found himself coming back to life.

"Is it over?" Susan asked.

"For now," Ev said dourly.

"So what do we do?"

"Start puttin' the pieces back together," Ev said, turning to Martin. "Son, how long do you think it'd take you to run down to the cave and fetch your brothers and sister?"

"Not long," Martin said, springing to his feet. "Keep the time and see."

Martin passed Ev the watch. A smile spread across both their faces. Then the boy scrambled off down the hillside, and Ev and Susan turned to the house.

"I remember places that looked like this up in Tennessee," Ev told Susan as they examined the shattered front window. "The cost of war."

"Yes," she said, glancing at Ben Wood's lifeless body ten yards away. "Is that what we had here, Ev? A war?"

"Of a sort," he said as he collected scattered fragments of glass and wood. "We were awful lucky. I was so scared Nolan would do something to you."

"I had my anxious moments," Susan admitted. "The worst part was hiding behind that door, not knowing what had become of you."

"It's goin' to be all right now," he promised. "The children will be home soon."

"I don't even have any plates left to serve dinner on," she said, suddenly giving way to tears. "Oh, Ev, they've broken everything. They ripped up our clothes, smashed my china cups, even emptied the straw from the mattresses."

"Mattresses can be refilled. We'll buy new clothes."

"And my grandmother's china? My music box?"

"They'll be missed," Ev admitted. "All things considered, it seems a small price. I'd gladly let them burn the house to the ground in order to have Rachel and the boys back here safe."

"I guess you're right, Ev. I'm just so angry!"

"I know," he said, kissing her forehead. "What we have to do now is clear away the rubble, tend the wounded, and rebuild."

Susan nodded, and they walked inside together and began clearing out space in the dining room. Soon the station became a small hospital. Mattresses were stuffed and set out. Art Hyland lay in the corner, his shoulder finally receiving proper attention. Tom Shipley and Parson Mills brought in the stage passengers next. Mrs. Bunting, the farmer's wife, sat in a chair beside the window mumbling to herself. Her dead husband lay in the stable, now converted to a morgue.

Dan Baker and Joe Gilbert were placed side by side along the wall. Baker said little, just moaned from the bullet in his side. Gilbert complained of the heat, of being shot, even of being late returning to Albany. Susan dressed the wound left by a bullet in the guard's wrist. The bullet itself had passed through cleanly. Gilbert's other wound, a bullet lodged in the back of his knee, would have to be tended later by a doctor in town.

As Susan turned her patients over to Tom Shipley for a moment, the sound of small feet on the porch outside attracted her attention.

"Ma! Pa!" Todd shouted, bursting through the doorway.

Susan lifted the boy off the ground and wrapped her

arms around his shuddering body. Rachel was only a few steps behind, and Ev hugged the girl, then carried her over to her mother. Finley arrived last, already busily spinning a tale of the night spent in the cave.

"You hungry, Todd?" Ev asked, taking the boy from Susan.

"I could eat a horse," Todd said. "But first I want to see the chickens. Did they get fed, Pa?"

"Yes," Ev said, laughing as he set Todd down.

"I'm starved," Finley announced, rushing to Ev's side and hugging his father.

"There's probably bread and smoked ham in the kitchen," Susan said, clutching Finley as tears rolled down her cheeks.

"Sure, Ma," Finley said, gazing up at the sadness in her eyes.

"It's good to have you home," Susan said, drawing them all to her side. "I missed you so."

Ev's eyes grew moist as he watched Susan and the children. They were his treasure, his cache of gold. And as he considered how close they'd all come to ending up like the farmer in the stable, he shook with rage.

"Pa?" Martin called from the porch. "Can I talk with you?"

"Sure, son," Ev said, leaving the children to their mother as he joined Martin outside.

"Pa, I came across Tim," Martin said sadly. "I was wonderin' if maybe we could. . ."

"Of course," Ev said, gripping Martin's shoulder. "Should we bring a horse?"

"It's not far," Martin said grimly. "I'll get a blanket. We can wrap him in it."

"See if you can find that old Indian blanket of mine," Ev suggested. "Tim always liked to wrap it around himself. I think he'd feel warm with it around him."

"Yeah," Marty said, sadly heading inside the house to locate the blanket.

"How 'bout I give you a hand with the horses?" Tom Shipley said, stepping down from the porch. "Don't see how we can get back on the trail today, but we ought to get those horses out of harness."

"In a bit," Ev said. "I've got one chore to attend to first."

"Want me to start by myself?" Shipley asked.

"Sure, but have Fin help. He knows which stalls to use and where to find liniment and brushes."

"I'm sure we'll do fine," Shipley said. "Must've been quite a strain these past few days, havin' a killer like Nolan around Susan and the kids."

"Yes."

"You did a fine job, today, Ev. The company's goin' to be grateful. I just wish we hadn't lost that payroll. But you kept us all from bein' slaughtered. If you hadn't hit that one on the roof, I don't know how we'd ever. . ."

"Sure," Ev said as Martin appeared with the blanket. "I've got that chore to attend to now, though."

Shipley moved aside as Ev followed Martin past the house. They walked a hundred yards through the trees to where Nolan's men had thrown young Tim Merritt's corpse. Martin stood close to his father as Ev gently lifted the cold, stiffened body. They then wrapped it in the blanket.

"When I got to the cave," Martin said as they started homeward, "all I could think of was how we'd all escaped, how lucky we'd been! Then I remembered Tim."

"I understand how you feel, son," Ev said. "I think about that gambler we buried, about young Tim and that farmer who had the bad luck to ride a coach the day George Nolan chose to rob it. Two men and one who had the right to grow into one. . . all dead. There's Art Hyland lyin' on his back with a blown up shoulder, Joe Gilbert likely lame, old Dan Baker shot half to pieces. And Nolan free to do it all again tomorrow."

"He won't have an easy time of it, Pa. Only one with him's Rip, and I don't know that Rip's got his heart in it anymore."

"I didn't see him stayin' behind to help Stacy or see that you were all right, Marty. Don't lose any sleep over that one! We're well rid of him."

"I know, Pa," Martin said somberly. "I was just, well, wonderin' if they don't feel like I did, trapped. I won't ever build another snare, Pa, or cage somethin' up."

"There's a difference, son," Ev said as they approached the station. "If Hazlewood and Nolan are locked up in a jail, it's because they earned it by their actions. They killed people. They stole what didn't belong to them. A man can't break the laws a people make and expect to get away with it. No, men like Nolan are the wolves of our world. They hunt anything and anybody, and they don't care what pain they cause. In the end, they'll find no refuge, no place to hide."

"I know," Martin said sadly. "I suppose that's why I'm sad for Rip. Because he's ridin' out there, knowin' it's bound to end soon."

"Just remember this," Ev said, trembling with anger. "He's ridin', Marty. This boy we're carryin' isn't. Tim was your friend! If there's sadness in your heart, save it for the one who deserves it."

They placed their lifeless bundle beside the stable, alongside Mr. Bunting. Tom Shipley and Fin had brought the first of the horses to its stall, and the animal had grown anxious at the smell of death, so the bodies had been taken outside. The Wood brothers and Lou Stacy lay a few feet away.

"Seems to me those two are too young to be dead," Parson Mills told Ev, pointing to the Woods. Can't be but seventeen, eighteen."

"They were old enough to threaten my wife and family," Ev snapped. "You'll find no kind words for them comin' from my lips."

"It's time to forgive, Everett," the preacher said. "It's the way of our faith."

"Maybe," Ev admitted, "but I can't. It's not in me, not with little Tim Merritt lyin' wrapped up in that blanket there. Too young? Tim's barely fourteen, hardly able to mount a horse without gettin' a hand up. Too young? The bullet that killed Tim came from a rifle in that one's hands," Ev added, pointing at the frozen face of Buck Wood. "A man kills. It's God's judgment he should die. An eye for an eye, the Bible says."

"I've never known you to be so bitter hard," Parson Mills said, shaking his head.

"There's never been a time like this," Ev explained wearily. "I've never watched my own children shake with fear, not knowin' if they'd see another mornin'."

Ev turned away from the preacher and walked to where Finley was helping Tom Shipley with the horses. Ev began unhitching the team. Work was the only true cure for anger. His hands wanted, needed something to do.

After the last animal was led to its stall, fed, brushed, and watered, Ev helped Susan begin the painful task of cleaning up the house. He discovered Mrs. Bunting and the children had cleared away most of the debris from the dining room and kitchen, but the stove needed to be settled back into its place, the pipe repaired, and shelves lay everywhere.

"It's hard to believe five men could do so much damage," Susan said as she swept the floor free of spilled flour and food scraps.

"Five men?" Ev said, rolling the words around in his mind. Three of them lay stone cold dead. Three others, too, killed because they'd had the misfortune to take the wrong stage or ride alone to return a stray horse. Three more were wounded.

"Pa!" Martin called from the porch.

"Yes, son," Ev answered, grabbing his rifle as he headed toward the front door.

"Mr. Merritt's here with Bob and Tom," Martin announced. "I thought maybe you'd. . ."

"Yes," Ev said. "It's my place to tell him."

Ev greeted Bill Merritt somberly.

"What's gone on here, Ev?" Merritt asked. "Tom brought word from Shipley you might have trouble, but it looks as though you've had a battle.

"We have," Ev said, steadying Merritt's horse. "Step down and talk, won't you?"

"Later," Merritt said, gawking at the broken front window, at the boxes of smashed china and glass. "First I'd like to see Tim. That's what brought us out here, Tim not coming in last night. Is he hereabouts?"

"He's here, Mr. Merritt," Martin said, leaning against the door.

"Glad to hear that!" Merritt said, smiling as he slid down from his saddle. His sons also dismounted. "I've been worried sick over that boy. Wait till I get him home."

"Bill," Ev said, gripping him firmly by the wrists. "Ever hear of a man named Nolan?"

"George Nolan?" young Tom gasped. "Road agent, robs banks."

"He's been here," Ev said.

"Is my Tim all right?" Merritt asked.

"He brought Marty's horse in yesterday mornin'. An act of kindness. Nolan had him shot."

"Shot?" Merritt asked, his hands shaking. "Well, is he all right? I've got to see him."

"He's. . . not. . . all right," Ev said, fighting to keep his lip from quivering. "God, Bill, I'd rather cut off my right hand than give you this news, but the boy's dead."

"Dead?" Merritt asked, his eyes swelling with tears. "Not Tim? He's only a boy, not as tall as a fencepost. Can't be!"

"He's over here," Ev said, leading the way past the stable to where the bodies lay. "If it's a comfort, he didn't suffer. I don't imagine he even knew what was happenin'."

"My Tim, dead? Oh, God, how am I going to tell his mama? Dead? Oh, Lord, how can it be?"

Ev led the way to where the Indian blanket cloaked the pale, cold face of Tim Merritt.

"There's been somethin' at it," Bill Merritt cried angrily when Ev pulled aside the blanket. "Animals!"

"Nolan had the body taken into the thicket," Ev explained. "Was only a short while back that Marty and I could bring it back. Parson Mills is here. He'd probably be glad to read some words, speak to the family."

"Tim's ma sets store by preachers," Merritt said. "I'll ask him by. You don't suppose I could have the loan of a horse, do you? I'd like to take the boy home."

"Surely," Ev agreed. "I know Marty'd like to come to the buryin'. Me, too, if you'll have me."

"It wasn't any of your doin'," Merritt said sadly. "I know you, Ev. If you could've stopped it, you would have. Come by 'round dusk. I always hated buryin' a child at dawn. Day's just beginnin' then. Seems too bright a moment."

"Dusk is good," Ev agreed. "That'll give us time to lay to rest the others."

"Who are they?" Merritt asked, gazing at the faces of the four corpses next to Tim. "One looks to be Lou Stacy."

"Is. He was one of Nolan's men. The older fellow is a farmer who was on the stage. The young one's are Nolan's nephews."

"You bury the farmer, Ev," Merritt said curtly. "Leave the others for the wolves like they left my Tim."

"I know how you feel," Ev said, clasping Bill Merritt's hands. "I thought for a time I was goin' to lose Susan, Marty, the little ones. It was a close thing, Bill. But I'd say they paid the price."

"And Nolan?" Merritt asked, as Susan walked up.

"Got away."

"I pray to God they'll answer for this!" Merritt roared. "I'd have Nolan hanged high!"

"He will be," Ev said coldly. "I promise you that, Bill."

"You promise?" Susan asked. "What do you mean promise, Ev?"

"I mean I'll see them caught."

"You're going after them," she said, covering her face.

"Tomorrow mornin'."

"I'll be ridin' with you, Mr. Raymond," nineteen-year-old Bob Merritt said.

"And I as well," Tom, a year younger, volunteered.

"You'll stay with your mama," Bill Merritt declared. "But I'll go, Ev."

"Bill, you're not so young as you once were," Ev objected.

"Would you allow another man to go after them that slew your boy?" Merritt asked. "No use arguing, Ev. I'll be going."

Ev nodded, then helped Martin bring a horse to carry Tim's body home.

The remnant of the afternoon passed. Evening came, marked by a violent red sunset. Ev and Tom Shipley dug three graves for Stacy and the Wood brothers off down the road. Ev thought it improper for the killers to lie beside the gambler. The farmer was wrapped in a shroud; Mrs. Bunting planned to have him laid in the family plot back home.

After a sparse dinner of ham and salted crackers, Ev led the way to the graves. He stood stone-faced while Parson Mills spoke words of forgiveness over the outlaws. Later the preacher talked of resurrection and hope as Tim Merritt's older brothers lowered him into a grave overlooking a grassy meadow.

Susan stood silently at Ev's side, speaking only a few comforting words to Sarah Merritt. As they rode wearily homeward, Ev felt the distance growing between them.

"Why are you going after them?" Susan asked that night as they lay together in their own bed for what seemed the first time in months. "You're not a marshal anymore. It's not your job. Send word to Mitch Burnett, let him tend to Nolan."

"The line's likely to offer a reward for the recovery of the payroll," Ev told her. "We're goin' to need the money to repair this place."

"Hang the money, Ev!" she cried. "That's got nothing to do with anything."

"You're right," he confessed. "I wasn't sure I would at first. . . . Then I realized I had to."

"Why?"

"So they'll never be able to do this to another man's family," Ev told her. "So no one will ever have to feel the pain Bill Merritt's feeling tonight because of George Nolan. So the children won't have nightmares that Nolan's back, so those nightmares can never become reality."

"I understand," she said, wiping her eyes. "I know what you feel. I just wish it wasn't always you."

"Me, too," he told her. "Me, too."

CHAPTER 17

EV was up early. There was something more precious and wonderful about each day now. He sat for a time at the edge of his bed, watching Susan sleep, gazing at her golden hair, at the softness that had managed to survive the harsh Texas winters and the trials of life on the frontier.

He then strolled through the house, ignoring broken chairs and dim hallways, bare walls stripped of the simple pictures and mementos that had made them part of a home. Instead he peered into the doorless rooms, smiled at little Rachel lying opposite the widow Bunting, warmed at the sight of Martin resting comfortably beside young Tom Shipley. Finley and Todd should have been there, too. But the streams of yellow light flooding the room had turned the boys into early risers.

Todd was with the chickens, chirping away like a sparrow at the birds, spreading feed and plucking eggs from under nesting hens. Ev envied the way a ten-year-old could so easily erase those dreadful days of captivity and return to the world of chickens and eggs, family and security.

Finley was busy filling the kindling box. Ev joined in, quietly collecting slivers of wood in his arms and carrying them to the box.

"I could get my ax, split some logs," Finley whispered.

"No, it's best we leave the others to sleep a bit longer," Ev said, motioning toward the dining room where Art Hyland, Dan Baker, and Joe Gilbert rested.

"You'll be leavin' soon," Finley said, leaning against Ev

a moment before pulling away. "You'll come back, though?"

"I always do," Ev said, reassuring the boy. "I promise, Fin, I won't stay gone long."

"It'll seem long, Pa. I remember. Ma won't say anything, but she'll worry. She'll take out her knittin' and work at it. Or else mend clothes. Marty'll ride out every night to watch the road, hopin' you'll be on your way home."

"That how it was at Jacksboro?"

"Mostly," Finley said. "Sometimes worse. Depends on who you were lookin' for. It wasn't so bad the time you were huntin' those card players. But this time. . . well, I figure Ma's goin' to fret somethin' awful. Be careful, Pa. That Nolan's mean. He wouldn't mind killin' you."

"I don't think I'll give him the chance then," Ev said, lifting Finley off the ground. "What do you see, Fin?"

"Not much," the boy said, grinning. "Todd and his chickens, the horses, you."

"Yeah," Ev said, returning Fin to the ground.

"What do you see, Pa?" Finley asked, gazing up into his father's tired, red-streaked eyes.

"Home," Ev told the boy. "Family."

It wasn't long before the others were awake. Ev saw to it the stovepipe was secure, then left the cooking of breakfast to Susan. With Martin's help, Ev got the fresh team hitched to the stage and the shrouded body of Mr. Bunting tied down on top.

"Figure Art's mended enough to drive the stage?" Shipley asked afterward.

"Maybe well enough to ride," Ev answered. "Wouldn't trust him to drive without bleedin' all over creation."

"Somebody ought to ride with you, Ev. I wish Joe. . ."

"Bill Merritt and his boy Bob are comin' along. You do this, though. When you pull into Albany, send word to Ft. Griffin. Get them to telegraph Nolan's description to the settlements up north. I'll see Mitch Burnett gets word, too."

"They've got a day's jump on you," Shipley pointed out. "You'll be hardpressed to cut 'em off."

"They won't have ridden far yesterday. They took no food with 'em, and th'only place nearby is Bill Merritt's ranch. We know they didn't go there."

"Ever consider they might head back here?"

"Then we'll cut 'em off," Ev said confidently. "I've tracked men before, Tom. I know what I'm about."

Shipley started to raise another objection, then reluctantly swallowed the words.

"If it was my family they'd held, I might do the same thing," Shipley admitted. "Watch yourself, though."

"I will."

Ev then led the way inside. Susan had fried slices of ham, then spread a pair of eggs on top. The breakfast was served on a slice of bread for lack of plates.

"Sorry we can't offer you anything grander," Susan told the guests. The children were sitting on a bench brought in from the stable. Only four chairs remained in one piece.

"Beats the squirrel stew we had at the Brazos crossin'," Joe Gilbert called from his bed four feet away. "Squirrels aren't bad eatin' sometimes, but three meals straight. . ."

"Started climbin' trees, huntin' acorns, huh?" Martin asked.

"Not too good at that just now," Joe said, glancing at his bandaged wrist and knee.

The breakfast conversation grew tense for a few moments as Mrs. Bunting spoke of her dead husband. But the widow suddenly changed topics, speaking with a stiffened lip of a new shop in Ft. Worth handling imported glassware. "I helped my daughter-in-law select a fine Bristol table service and crystal straight from Ireland," Mrs. Bunting told Susan.

"You wouldn't happen to know if they carried anything

from Norway, would you?" Susan asked, glancing at the shattered hutch.

"Why, yes, I believe they did," Mrs. Bunting replied. "I'll leave you the address. Perhaps Mr. Raymond can take you there."

Susan looked over at Ev and smiled. He nodded, then excused himself from the table.

Ev paced back and forth on the porch for several minutes. He could hear the children clearing the table. There were no plates to wash, but tin coffee cups needed scrubbing. Before Susan began organizing the clean-up, she stepped outside.

"It's strange," she said as she handed Ev a flour sack filled with provisions. "I thought we'd said our last farewell."

"This isn't a farewell," Ev told her, wrapping an arm around her. "I'll be gone such a short time you'll hardly have a chance to miss me."

"There's no time that short," Susan said, gripping his arm so tightly Ev thought it might come off.

"I won't be long, Susan."

"You used to say that when you'd leave Jacksboro. Ev, I thought we'd be safe out here, that you wouldn't have to do this anymore. But I guess we're never really certain of anything."

"No," Ev agreed.

They stood together as Tom Shipley announced it was time the stage was leaving. Parson Mills helped Mrs. Bunting along. Art stumbled along behind them. Ev left Susan long enough to help young Tom carry Dan Baker to the coach. Marty helped Joe Gilbert.

"I'll pass on the word, Ev," Shipley promised as he released the brake and got the horses in motion. The stage rolled along then, vanishing westward into swirls of dust.

"I guess you'll be leaving now," Susan whispered to Ev.

"It's time," he told her. "I'd best see the children."

Susan nodded, and he slipped inside the doorway. Rachel was busy wiping a cloth across the table. Todd was dragging the three mattresses from the dining room.

"You leavin', Pa?" Todd asked, stopping long enough to gaze up at his father.

"Shortly," Ev said.

Rachel rushed over, and Ev hugged her tightly. Todd stepped closer, and Ev pulled the boy over as well.

"I won't be long," Ev promised. "Mind your ma."

"We will," Todd pledged.

"Look after yourselves, too," Ev added as he stepped away.

"We will."

Martin and Finley were at the corral. They had Coffee, the brownish-colored stallion, saddled and waiting.

"We've had practice, remember?" Martin reminded Ev.

"I remember," Ev said, tying his provision bag behind the blanket roll. "Look after your ma."

"We've had practice at that, too," Fin added. "Don't worry, Pa. We know what's to be done."

"I ought to go with you," Martin said. "I'm fourteen. Don't say that's not old enough, Pa. It's as old as Tim's ever goin' to be."

"I won't say you're too young, son," Ev replied quietly. "But there's always the outside chance Nolan might double back around. I feel better knowin' you're here."

"That's not the reason," Marty grumbled. "I won't say goodbye again, Pa."

"Then say adios," Ev suggested. "Know what it means?"

"It's Spanish," Finley said.

"Means 'go with God'," Marty explained. "Paco Ruiz used to say it."

"Tell me that, boys," Ev said, mounting the horse. "Adios."

"Adios, Pa," Finley said sadly.

"Adios, Pa," Marty echoed.

Ev turned the horse away from the house. Always before he'd paused, taking a last, reluctant glance at his home. This time he rode steadily northward, afraid to hestitate, to delay.

"I know you, Nolan," Ev said to the wind. "I remember. You always head north, don't you?"

In his mind Ev drew a map of the wild, rolling hill country that spread northward toward the Red River. There were few towns and fewer ranches. It wasn't long ago the Comanches ruled those hills. Nobody made good time across that land, nobody. And except for game, there'd be no food.

He met Bill Merritt and young Bob near a hill studded with live oaks. Ev had tracked Nolan and Hazlewood that far the night before.

"They appear to be headed north," Merritt said.

"That's how Nolan usually travels," Ev said. "It's good fortune for us. The Brazos is flooded. He'll have a time findin' a crossing."

"Might swim across," Bob said.

"Those ponies he took grow fretful near water," Ev explained. "Might find himself afoot. There's another possibility, though. He might follow the river back east. We'd be wise to warn Mitch Burnett at Brazos Crossin'. He can have men cover that direction.

Merritt nodded.

"Bob, you know the way there?" Ev asked. "Think you can find Sheriff Burnett?"

"Yes, sir," Bob answered.

"It's for you to say, Bill," Ev said, turning to Bob's father, "but it needs doin'."

"Ride to the crossing, Bob," Bill Merritt instructed his son. "Then meet us at Shaw's."

Bob nodded and started his horse eastward.

"I was thinkin' of Shaw's myself," Ev admitted. "Sooner or later they'll wind up there."

"So, we head there, do we?"

"After a fashion," Ev said. "Let's follow their trail awhile. I wouldn't want Nolan backtrackin' on us."

"No," Merritt agreed. "He's been tracked before. Each time he's slipped away like a renegade Comanche. Tricky, that one."

"Yes, but you and I know this country," Ev said confidently. "Sooner or later he'll turn to the river, swing along to Shaw's. I'll find him."

"We'll do it together," Bill Merritt insisted. "I believe you'd have to agree my injury's been at least as great as your own."

"Yes," Ev agreed.

So on they rode together, two avenging angels bent on bringing George Nolan to a long-delayed Judgment Day.

CHAPTER 18

EV had no real trouble locating Nolan's trail. An hour after leaving the station, Ev spotted the tracks of two shod ponies in the soft sand of the plain. Few riders crossed that wild unbroken land, and those mustangs which still ran free wore no shoes.

"Look there," Ev said, pointing out the trail to Bill Merritt.

"Looks like they were movin' fast," Merritt observed.

"Heavy in the saddle, too," Ev added. "Must be the money. They didn't have any food with 'em."

Ev dismounted in order to examine the tracks more closely. It was hard to tell when Nolan and Hazlewood had passed through there, but it was easy to tell where they were headed. The sea of buffalo grass which dotted the landscape revealed a distinct path where the horses had passed.

"They're headed for the river," Merritt declared as he followed Ev's actions. "For the trees."

"I've done the same in strange country," Ev recalled. "Trees usually mean water."

"My papa used to have a sayin'," Merritt said as Ev climbed atop Coffee. "The land tells a hundred stories. The trick is readin' the right one."

Ev nodded as he led the way not to the north, not to Shaw's Crossing a mere five or six miles away, but westward toward the tree-lined hills.

You've made your fatal mistake, Nolan, Ev silently told the outlaw. You don't know this land, *my* land. You held the upper hand once, but now it's my turn.

"When I first came to this country, the buffalo ran this range in their thousands," Merritt said. "Comanches, too. They burned us out three, four times. My folks wanted to leave, but Sarah's papa said the Comanches would pass off the page, so to speak. The buffalo swung westward as the cattle moved in. Later the hunters whittled away at the herds."

"Time marches on," Ev said.

"I used to take the boys up into those hills. I believe Tim liked it best of all. My, did he love those Comanche stories of his grandpapa."

"He used to talk me into spinnin' a tale or two," Ev said, smiling as he recalled Tim's eager eyes.

"I saw you wrapped him in that blanket. He sure had a fondness for it. Used to pester me somethin' awful to ride up to Ft. Griffin and see if I could talk one of those Tonkawa scouts out of one. It's a kindness you puttin' him in that. He's restin' in it still."

"I liked that boy," Ev said gently.

"He was a good one. He'll be missed. Strange thing, havin' your children go before you. Sarah and I lost two girls 'fore they were five. One fell from the loft. Th'other caught a fever, was gone 'fore we knew it. Tim's the first of the boys, though. It's different somehow, him being the youngest."

"Life's cold cruel sometimes," Ev said, staring off into the distant hills. "My pa had four sons. I'm all that's left. Two fell in battle. Finley, the youngest, was out checkin' stock. Fifteen, I suppose at the time. Comanches swept down on him. Boy didn't have a chance. I named my second boy for him."

"It's a fine way to remember him," Merritt said, coughing. "Maybe Bob or Tom'll do that for my. . . little. . . Tim."

Ev slowed the pace a bit. He could tell Bill Merritt rode only with great effort. The old rancher couldn't have slept many hours, and Tim's death weighed heavily.

"Guess you've tracked killers plenty of times," Merritt said as they approached the hills.

"More times than I care to remember," Ev said, wiping the sweat from his forehead. "Thought I was finished a couple of times."

"Oh?"

"You ever hear 'bout the dog chased a possum three days and three nights? Well, he found out it wasn't a possum. Caught himself the biggest, meanest brown bear in tarnation! Next thing you knew, it was the bear chasin' that dog."

"I had a wolf turn on me once, Ev. In those same hills up there. You figure Nolan might try that?"

"Hard to tell," Ev admitted. "Hill country's not the best territory for trackin'. But I'd say he hasn't had his full run yet. You know game. They run till they tire. Then they start thinkin'."

"Sure would be better to catch him out here in the open."

"That won't happen," Ev told his companion. "No, Nolan's in those hills already. But he hasn't eaten anything. Hasn't got a lot of ammunition. Likely, he's short on sleep. He's used to a gang, too, only now he's close to alone."

Yes, Ev thought. Tired and hungry, scared, with me on his trail. He's close to desperate. I know just how he feels. I've been there a hundred times since the eastbound pulled in.

"When do you expect to close with him?" Merritt asked.

"Before tonight," Ev answered. "His ponies won't run far today, not after bein' idle all that time in the corral and then ridden hard yesterday. Could be they've pulled up lame."

"If it was me, I'd lay myself a nice little ambush up there."

"It's the place for it," Ev agreed. "We'll see soon enough."

Actually, though, it was nearly midday when they left

the range. The trail almost disappeared on the rocky slopes of the sandstone hills, but here and there Ev noticed a bent juniper branch or a fragment of torn clothing.

"They'd be at Shaw's by now if they'd stayed north," Merritt said, amused at the thought of Nolan and Hazlewood riding blindly into the endless hills, searching for some sign of the river when in fact the trees were fed by springs.

"I've given that some thought, Bill," Ev said, drawing his horse to a halt. "Even a stranger's bound to figure the river's on beyond these hills. Nolan's bound to swing north after a time. First crossing he'd reach would be Shaw's. You could wait him out there."

"And you?"

"I'd make sure he kept north and west, didn't circle back to your place. Or mine."

"I told you before," Merritt said, taking a sip from his water flask. "I'll see Tim's killers hung. Or shoot 'em down myself."

"Climbin' hills is hard work, though," Ev pointed out. "And if they slip on out to Shaw's before Bob gets there. . . Don't forget. Shaw's got a wife and children, too."

"I'll stay, Ev. If I come to the point I can't keep pace, I'll leave. Fair enough?"

"Never asked more of anyone."

The truth was, though, Bill Merritt was struggling even then. His horse lacked Coffee's strength. As the sun hung high overhead, Ev signalled a break. They ate their lunch, and Ev scouted the ground ahead.

"You know this country, Bill?" Ev asked when he finished.

"Fair," Merritt said.

"As I remember, there's a kind of a canyon just ahead. Looks for all the world to be a road due north."

"Quarter of a mile ahead maybe."

"If you were Nolan, tired and hungry, wonderin' if you'd ever find the river, wouldn't you try a route like that?"

Merritt nodded, then frowned.

"I see what you're thinkin', Ev," Merritt said. "If you could circle around, get above them. Problem is, there's not any way. That canyon cuts through these hills for five, six miles. Only way to the other side is up from Shaw's. No way to beat Nolan there."

"Then we've got trouble," Ev said, sighing. "We could end up bein' the ones to get ambushed. They're ahead of us. They could be up there, watchin', hopin' we'll come that way."

"They don't know how deep the canyon is."

"They will when they get through it, Bill. They'll do that before we catch 'em."

"We'll keep our guard up, Ev. Watch for rockslides. That's a sign somethin' is up there above you."

"Yes," Ev agreed. But when you know they're up there, it's too late, he told himself.

As they resumed their quest, Ev discovered Nolan had indeed seen the canyon. Two clear sets of tracks appeared in the narrow, sandy bottom of the canyon. The steep walls up either side were an obstacle no horse could overcome. But as the canyon twisted and turned, numerous ambush points appeared. Each time Ev would slowly, cautiously move ahead. But no one ever appeared. No one fired.

No, not yet, he told himself as they continued. But what about next time? Death often came quickly, with a suddenness that left no time for farewell letters or carefully drawn documents. He wished he'd held Susan longer. He wished he'd said more to Martin, hugged Finley as he'd embraced Todd and Rachel.

"They're getting tired," Merritt said, pointing to the tracks.

Ev nodded. The ponies were slowing. The tracks were deeper, and the fore and hind feet drew closer together.

I wonder what he's thinking? Ev asked himself. Is he planning something? Maybe he's located a hiding place.

Suddenly Ev drew in his reins and halted his horse. The two sets of tracks continued, but one set was far less deep.

"Be careful," Ev whispered to Merritt. "In a minute, I want you to ride past me, hard, like your life depended on it."

"What's wrong?" Merritt asked.

"No time to explain," Ev said, drawing his rifle from its scabbard.

"Are they up there?"

"We'll find out soon," Ev said, yelling, "Now!"

Merritt slapped his horse into a gallop. At the same instant, Ev slid down from Coffee and let the stallion choose his own path. A rifle shot rang out, and the canyon echoed with its sound. The bullet slammed against the rocky canyon wall ten feet from where Ev scurried along. It might well have passed through his skull had he remained atop his horse.

"Ev?" Merritt called from up ahead.

"Hold onto my horse!" Ev shouted as he huddled behind a boulder. Another shot tore through the air a few feet away.

"You all right?" Merritt called out.

"Sure! They split up," Ev explained. "Try to follow the one with the horses. He'll have the money."

"And you?"

"I'll tend to this one on the hillside," Ev said, examining the steep slope. A jagged outcropping shielded a path up the canyon wall. Ev flinched as a third shot struck the rocks behind him. Then he raced toward the outcropping, arriving only seconds before a fourth shot struck the ground behind him.

"You've got more tricks than a Brazos rattler, Raymond!" George Nolan exclaimed from above. "Thought you'd be dead for sure by now."

"How you feelin' up there, Nolan?" Ev asked. "Hungry? Thirsty? Miss your nephews any?"

"I miss your wife's cookin'," Nolan mocked.

"Not me. I just had some soft, tender ham, a slice of bread, drank all the water I wanted."

"You're a demon! How'd you catch up so fast?"

"You always head north," Ev explained. "I saw you were makin' for these hills. It was the trees, wasn't it? A fool's move, Nolan. Only water hereabouts is underground."

"What!"

"Oh, there's a spring or two a mile and a half back. But you'll never see it. I cut you off from your horse."

"Don't forget about Rip. He'll be back to help."

"Will he?" Ev asked. "Like you helped Lou Stacy? He learns quickly, that Rip. He's had a good teacher. Look after yourself. Isn't that what you told him, Nolan? He's got the money, too."

Ev could tell by the silence that drifted across the canyon that his words had an effect. Slowly, carefully, he began his ascent up the canyon wall. The outcropping provided a perfect cover. Nolan fired off a wild shot from time to time. But he'd seen no target.

He'll never know where I came from, Ev told himself. He'll be half-crazed from hunger.

Ev pictured himself standing beside the gallows as Mitch Burnett motioned for the trap door to be sprung. Nolan would drop like a fifty-pound sack of flour, near snapping the rope. The feet would kick, once, twice maybe. That'd be all, and Nolan would be dead.

"Where are you, Marshal?" Nolan snarled in a dozen directions, firing wildly at shadows. "Come on! We'll settle this, just you and me."

You're right, Ev said silently. It will be just you and me. But it will be on my terms, not yours.

When Ev eventually reached the crest of the canyon wall, he slithered like a snake through the rocks and trees. Nolan was just ahead, firing down at rocks or bushes.

"Come on out, Marshal!" Nolan barked. "Show yourself!"

Ev only smiled and closed the distance. It was down to thirty, then twenty feet. Finally, with Nolan squarely in his sights, Ev spoke quietly.

"Looks like your run's about up, Nolan!"

The outlaw froze. The rifle in his great bear-like hands shook noticeably.

"You never should've come up here, Marshal!" Nolan growled, never looking in Ev's direction. "This is my game."

"Is it now?" Ev mocked. "We'll see about that. Drop the rifle!"

"Can't do that."

"You don't, you're dead where you stand," Ev declared. "I wouldn't count on much patience from me."

"You remember Rip Hazlewood, though," Nolan said. "He's just behind you."

"Is he?" Ev asked, tensing.

"Sure is. Why, this very moment he's. . ."

Nolan never finished the sentence. Instead he spun around and raised his rifle. Ev fired instinctively, once, twice, three times in all. The bullets smashed into Nolan's belly and chest. The rifle trickled from Nolan's fingers, careening wildly down the slope.

"Rip?" Nolan called out.

"You knew he wasn't there," Ev said. "I would've brought you to trial, Nolan!"

"And then hung me?" Nolan gasped, his eyes blazing wildly as he struggled to reach the pistol in his gunbelt. "No, I'll never stretch a rope."

"No, I'd say you were finished, all right."

"Funny," Nolan said, sinking to one knee and coughing

blood. "I don't do a lot of misjudgin'. Misjudged you. Young Rip, too."

Nolan bellowed as he regained his feet. Pain flooded his face as he screamed wildly. Then, his fingers still fighting to grip the handle of his Colt, Nolan lurched backwards, over and down into the depths of the canyon, his death cry tearing the air and echoing through the hills.

"So, Hazlewood," Ev said, gazing northward toward the far entrance of the canyon. "You heard your uncle's call. You're next."

With that said, Ev started down the steep hillside, as determined as ever to end the nightmare, to finish what he'd begun seemingly in another lifetime.

"So that's Nolan," Bill Merritt said when Ev reached the canyon floor.

"That's him," Ev said, turning the shattered body of the outlaw face up.

"I saw his horse up ahead," Merritt went on to say. "No saddlebags. Suppose we ought to take the body back."

"There's a reward," Ev reminded his friend.

"Personally I'd as soon leave him out here to the wolves," Bill Merritt raged. "Let 'em chew on him the way they did my boy. But I'd hate to spoil your chance at the reward."

"You're due a share," Ev said.

"No, I could never take money for what I'm doin', and I heard Susan talkin' about your place. You'll need the money. Let's go. That other one can't have gotten far."

"No," Ev agreed as he started after Nolan's horse. Hazlewood wouldn't know where to hide. His mask had always been his smile, those easy manners. No, he wouldn't even make it to Shaw's. He'll end up on some hillside, nestled in with those saddlebags full of banknotes.

Ev fought off a grin. No man should deal out death with a smile. There should be a grimness, a reluctance. But as he remembered Nolan holding a knife to Todd, coldly shooting down the gambler, kicking Art Hyland, and opening up on the stage, Ev found no sympathy. It wasn't possible. All the softness, the compassion had been killed by a living, breathing nightmare. And it wouldn't be over until Rip Hazlewood was accounted for.

CHAPTER 19

IT took but a few minutes to wrap George Nolan in a blanket and tie him across his saddle. The horse stirred nervously, and Ev stroked its lathered neck.

"Horse's about spent," Ev observed.

"Feet seem sound," Merritt said, running his gnarled hands along the pony's legs.

"I wish we could leave him here to rest," Ev said, "but Hazlewood's just ahead."

"Mustang's a rare creature," Merritt declared as he mounted his horse. "Sometimes you'd swear he couldn't take another step. But he keeps on comin'."

Yes, Ev thought as he handed the reins of Nolan's horse to Bill Merritt and climbed into the saddle. That's the way on the frontier. You don't give in. You go till you drop.

As they continued onward, following Hazlewood's trail toward the river, Ev fought off the weariness that was setting in. He knew Hazlewood was just as tired, and a hunter who relaxed the pressure on his quarry sometimes lost it altogether. If they didn't let up, Hazlewood would grow careless, reckless.

"Tell me 'bout this one that's left, Ev," Merritt asked as they rode.

"Rip Hazlewood," Ev muttered. "He was on the westbound last week. Stayed at the station, said he was waitin' on cousins. But he was there to scout the station, set up the robbery."

A vision of Hazlewood grinning as George Nolan arrived sprouted in Ev's mind. Other memories followed, Hazlewood firing on the stage, rummaging through the

house. . . softer ones, too. The sight of Hazlewood helping Finley and Todd paint the stable.

"I've seen that kind before," Merritt said, shaking his
head. "Snake in the grass. Slithers along so you get used
to him. Then he up and bites you in the leg."

"I suppose," Ev replied. But the recollection that remained after all the others passed was of the young gunman gazing at Martin, watching the children escape,
holding the rifle that might have dealt death so easily.

I could go back, Ev thought. But the law wasn't written
for a man's convenience. There was the money to consider. And Tim Merritt.

Hazlewood's trail wound through the soft sand that
covered the gentle grade down toward the river. But soon
the tracks swung around to the west, weaving erratically
into the hills. There was no pattern to the movements.

"He's wily, that one," Merritt declared. "Knows he can't
keep going much farther, so he's keeping us guessing,
trying to last till dark."

"Might just do it, too," Ev said as the sun began to set.
"Tomorrow's another day altogether."

"Ev, you think we ought to keep after him? I'm not such
a fair shot when the light fades."

"We could make camp," Ev said. "Fact is, you could go
along to Shaw's, take Nolan along. Bob's likely there."

"You're not considering going after that one alone, are
you?"

"No. I'll just make my camp up high so I can watch the
river. I wouldn't want him slippin' past me."

"It's a good hour to Shaw's."

"If you're goin', best start on along."

"I will," Merritt said, extending his hand to Ev. "We'll
be along toward morning."

"I'll wait for you atop the hill," Ev said, clasping Merritt's hand, then nodding farewell.

Ev watched Merritt head on toward the river, then stroked Coffee's weary neck.

"There," Ev whispered, pointing to what appeared to be a clearing above a sharp bend of the river. "I'll wait there."

It took but half an hour to complete the climb up the hill. Hazlewood's trail vanished as the sand gave way to stone. But Ev knew the outlaw was near, sensed his presence.

"It's not my doin'," Ev spoke as he slid wearily from the saddle. "But tomorrow we'll be settlin' this."

Ev dared not build a fire, so he contented himself with a supper of cold meat and raw carrots. As night fell, Ev's thoughts turned toward Antelope Springs, toward Susan and the children. He smiled as he dreamed of Martin and Finley working the horses, of Todd chirping away with his chickens, of Rachel aiding her mother in the house.

Ev thought also of the work that lay ahead rebuilding the house. New glass for the broken windows would come high. The reward for Nolan stood at five hundred dollars, Ev recalled. If the money could be recovered, the line would likely prove generous. If not, it was possible the route could even change, leaving Ev short of funds to pay off the note.

That was the real nightmare, owing money he couldn't pay. There weren't many jobs around for a man closing in on his fortieth birthday. He dreaded telling Susan they must leave, take up the wandering life of a hired hand or deputy marshal. And if the word got out Rip Hazlewood had dusted Ev off, gotten safely away to Kansas or Mexico, there'd be few offers of lawman's work.

Terrible doubts haunted Ev's dreams. Loneliness penetrated to his very heart. Morning found him cold, lost and alone. But as he pulled on his boots and prepared to rejoin the Merritts, he shook off the doubts. All that remained to be done was track down one young outlaw, and

Ev had done it a hundred times.

Bill and Bob Merritt arrived a little after eight. They'd swapped out horses at Shaw's, and both seemed ready, eager even, to settle the matter at hand. Ev mounted Coffee and joined them at the river's edge.

"Left Nolan's body at Shaw's," Bill Merritt said. "We'll pick up your horse on the swing back home."

"I appreciate that," Ev said. "Now I guess it's time to finish this."

"I suppose I rode all the way to Brazos Crossin' for nothin'," Bob said, scratching his cheek. "Appears you and Pa've cut 'em off."

"Didn't know that when I sent you," Ev explained. "It's always best to take precautions."

As they picked up Hazlewood's trail on the far hillside, Ev took more precautions. He kept young Bob on the left flank, preventing an ambush. Bob's father watched the far bank of the river in case Hazlewood somehow managed a crossing. Ev himself did most of the tracking. Then, as the three of them followed the river's sharp turn, they saw Hazlewood's horse limping beside the river.

"Keep a sharp eye out!" Ev hollered, advancing cautiously to the pony. The horse was soaked through. Hazlewood had tried to swim the river, no doubt. The outlaw'd failed, leaving his horse lame and himself trapped.

"Can't be far," Bill Merritt declared. "This horse is still wet."

Ev nodded, then searched the saddle for some sign of the money. The saddlebags were gone, though. But not far.

"Well, Marshal!" a voice cried out from behind a pile of boulders up ahead. "Figured you'd be by."

"Come on out of there, Hazlewood," Ev said, pulling out his rifle and readying a shot. "You can't hope to slip away now. You've got no horse."

"No, he's pulled up lame," Hazlewood said. " I could buy one off you maybe. I've got cash, lots of it."

"You'd do well to turn loose of that money," Ev instructed. "I'm surprised your Uncle George let it out of his sight."

"Well, he wasn't exactly figurin' on me leavin'," Hazlewood admitted. "I was supposed to come along behind you. But we didn't know you'd have help. That changed things some."

"Especially for your uncle," Ev pointed out.

"He dead?"

"Dead as a man can get. Turned him in at Shaw's Crossin'."

"So, there is a crossin' nearby," Hazlewood said. "Thought so. Never did think much of the odds of travelin' foreign country."

"You've got no chance of escape!" Ev shouted. "Why not give it up? I'll see you have your trial."

"Oh, I'm sure of that, Marshal. Don't suppose if I tossed you the payroll, you could look th'other way?"

"Can you think of any reason I should?" Ev asked. "And what about these others? You know who they are? The father and brother of that boy Buck shot down."

"Makes it hard, doesn't it?" Hazlewood shouted. "Still, I judge you owe me."

"What?"

"Know what the time is, Marshal?"

Ev pulled out his watch and read the dial.

"That's right!" Hazlewood reminded him. "I kept that safe for you. And that's not all. There's Marty and the little ones as well. That's a heavy debt to pay, Marshal."

"I thought of that," Ev said, sliding down from his saddle. "But it doesn't erase what you've done. Might get you off with a lighter sentence."

"Well, that's dandy, Marshal!" Hazlewood complained. "I save your kids, and you still mean to bring me in! Well,

Ma always did say I'd wind up on the short end of a rope."

Ev dove to the ground as Hazlewood opened fire. Coffee reared up on his hind legs and scrambled away. Bill Merritt retreated also. Bob dismounted and answered the fire.

Ev crept forward, carefully shielding himself behind the trees and rocks that cluttered the river bottom. Hazlewood fired rapidly at first, then grew conservative. Ev suspected ammunition might be running low.

Ev didn't catch a glimpse of Hazlewood for several moments. The outlaw had managed to crawl away from his original position. The saddlebags remained.

"You could tell 'em I drowned," Hazlewood pleaded. "I can't do you any harm out here."

Ev stared at the trail Hazlewood had left. One leg had been dragged along, likely broken in the attempt to ford the river. It was tempting to turn away, leave the crippled young man to the whims of nature, to hungry wolves and slow starvation.

"Don't suppose you'd consider lookin' th'other way?" Hazlewood called out.

"I don't see Bill Merritt goin' along with it even if I did," Ev answered.

"I'm sorry about that boy," Hazlewood cried out, a trace of desperation appearing in his voice for the first time. "I never took a hand in it. I tried to talk Uncle George out of it. God knows I never shot a kid."

"Might as well have," Bob called out.

"No luck, eh?" Hazlewood asked. "Well, I had a fair ride while it lasted. Guess that's all a man can ask for."

Hazlewood made a sudden break for the brush. Ev aimed and fired in an instant, and Hazlewood screamed out in pain. The bullet had struck his lame leg.

"Can't you at least shoot straight, Marshal!" Hazlewood cried. "Don't leave me crippled! Don't haul me to trial in a basket. Finish the job!"

Ev edged forward cautiously. The outlaw was hurt, but a limp leg was far from fatal.

"Give up, Hazlewood!" Ev urged as he finally fixed the outlaw in the sights of the Winchester. "Give up!"

"What'd be waitin' for me?" Hazlewood shouted, raising himself with the help of a nearby oak branch. "Hangin'? Jail at best! One death's as good as another!"

"Don't!" Ev shouted as Hazlewood slowly raised his rifle. "Don't!"

Ev ducked as the outlaw fired. A limb inches away shattered. A second shot whined overhead.

There's nothing left to do, Ev sighed as he aimed his rifle. He fired, and the young outlaw gazed upward, then fell.

CHAPTER 20

EV found no satisfaction in wrapping Rip Hazlewood in a blanket. The youthful bandit's eyes seemed still to be pleading for another chance.

"Can't you look the other way?" Hazlewood's voice repeated over and over in Ev's mind, echoing until the noise seemed to split him in half.

"Guess you'll be glad to be gettin' along home," Bill Merritt said as he helped Ev tie the body onto Coffee's back. The other horse had a pulled tendon. The poor animal would be lucky to limp to Shaw's. It was only half a mile, and Ev knew he could lead Coffee that far.

"Mitch Burnett'll be there by now," Bob told them. "There's another man that'll be glad there's no more George Nolan ridin' around."

"Yes, it's over," Ev said, sliding his rifle into its scabbard.

The Merritts accompanied Ev back to Shaw's Crossing, but they didn't stay long.

"You're due a share of the reward," Ev reminded Bill.

"No, you did the shooting, Ev," Merritt declared. "Me, well, I just came along to see justice done, my boy's killing paid for."

"Now there's nothin' left for us to tend to," Bob said. "You settle everything with Sheriff Burnett. If you need witnesses, he knows where we can be found."

Ev nodded, then waved good-bye as Bill turned away southward, toward home.

Yes, home, Ev thought as he led Coffee to the hitching rack outside Shaw's store. That's what this was all about, making the station a home again, chasing away the shadows of those past few days, laying to rest the nightmares of the children.

"I see you got th'other one, too," Mitch said, stepping through the door as Ev flung the saddlebags over one shoulder. "Know his name?"

"Hazlewood," Ev told the sheriff. "Rip Hazlewood. Another one of Nolan's nephews."

"That finishes it, doesn't it?"

"Yes," Ev said sadly. "I brought in the payroll."

"If you feel up to the responsibility, it'd be easiest for you to take it back to Antelope Springs. There's another coach due in a few days, right?"

Ev scratched his head and tried to recall the schedule. If Martin was there, the boy would have known.

"I'll take it home with me," Ev agreed.

"Shaw's got your horse grazin' in his pasture," Burnett explained. "We buried Nolan up a ways. Guess this other one'd want to be close by."

"Seems fittin'," Ev said. "He followed his uncle to the grave. Might as well follow him the rest of the way."

They left the saddlebags with Shaw. Then Mitch Burnett grabbed a spade and accompanied Ev back outside. Ev led Coffee along until they reached a mound of earth marked by a simple plank marker.

"Didn't know if he'd want a cross," Burnett said. "Didn't seem likely, not with shootin' little Tim Merritt. Plank's easier, too."

"Don't guess there's anyone around to remember," Ev said as the sheriff began digging. "Certainly no one's left who'd mourn. But seems like there ought to be," Ev said, loosening the ropes that held Hazlewood to the saddle. "Everyone ought to have someone miss him."

"Don't expect any tears from me, Ev," Burnett said, stopping long enough to catch his breath. "I remember the night Timmy Merritt was born. He wet his britches sittin' on my knee. Why, the times I rocked him to sleep! That boy was worth fifty George Nolans."

"Maybe," Ev said, dragging Hazlewood's body from the horse.

Mitch Burnett lifted the blanket long enough to stare into Hazlewood's lifeless eyes.

"Wonder what leads the young ones to take up with the likes of Nolan?" Burnett asked. "I've seen it a hundred times. Those old killers attract 'em like a flower draws bees."

"I suppose part of it was the war," Ev said, taking over the digging. "Boys lost their pas. Then they listen to all that foolishness about cavalry charges and eternal glory! I rode for Bedford Forrest, and we made a lot of charges, Mitch. I never saw any glory, just a lot of shootin' and a lot of cold, hard death."

"Could be," Burnett agreed. "I guess a lot of 'em's farmers, boys bred to long days of hard work. They see a chance at somethin' quick and easy. They hear about a stage carryin' ten thousand dollars. That's more cash money than their pa's goin' to see in his lifetime. So they buy a gun and make their bid."

Ev sighed and devoted his full attention to the grave. He was dead-tired, and his arms felt as though they were weighted down by fifty-pound sacks of grain. Only the dream of returning home. . . to Susan and the children kept him at his task.

"Ever think of givin' up the law?" Ev asked as he finally completed the trench a while later.

"Take up a stage station like you, Ev?" Burnett asked, laughing. "No, I guess I'm too old to learn somethin' new. I kind of like the wide open spaces. I'll admit the nights get cold and lonely sometimes, and I envy you Susan and the kids. But I'd never make a go of settlin' down. Too much wild mustang in me, I guess."

They dropped Hazlewood's body in the grave, then began covering it with dirt.

"You ever miss your marshalin' days?" Burnett asked when they'd finished. "Stagecoaches must seem a little tame by comparison."

"Not lately," Ev said. "I do sometimes. Jack County was home for a lot of years. But Susan wasn't happy there. It's nice lookin' in on the little ones at night, seein' 'em grow taller, hearin' their prayers, and sharin' their dreams."

"Sounds like you're sold on it," Burnett said as he led the way back to Shaw's.

"Yes," Ev said, smiling as thoughts of home filled the cold emptiness that had been growing inside him since setting out after Nolan and Hazlewood the day before.

Shaw had a celebration of sorts planned, but Ev left Mitch Burnett to drink away the afternoon. Ev retrieved the saddlebags and set off southward. An image of Susan and the kids nestled around the hearth on a cold December's eve kept Ev going as he rode homeward on Coffee, leading the other pony along, anxious to see the little station again. Coffee seemed to sense the urgency in Ev's heart. Even the poor pony, ridden to near exhaustion by George Nolan, trotted along homeward with renewed energy.

It was near nightfall when Ev spotted the faint outline of the buildings in the distance. He was dusty and tired and nigh spent. Still, the place seemed precious, more beautiful in its shabbiness than a glittering royal palace.

"Pa!" Finley cried out from the bottom of Calvary Hill. "Pa's back!"

Ev felt his legs grow lighter, and he nudged Coffee into a trot.

"Pa's home!" another voice, and another called out from the station.

Home, Ev thought as he paused long enough for Finley to lift himself up onto his father's lap. Yes, that was what mattered above everything.

"Glad you got back all right," Finley said, wrapping his skinny arms around Ev's waist and squeezing tightly.

"I thought you'd gotten used to this," Ev said, stroking the boy's chest as he slowed Coffee for the ascent up the hill.

"Me, too," Fin said, trembling slightly. "Guess I'm too old to be ridin' up here with you."

"Oh, I'd say twelve can get by with it now and then."

"Ma cried a lot last night," the boy whispered.

"I know," Ev said. "I guess we never really get very used to being apart."

"Guess not," Fin agreed.

When Ev reached the top of the hill, he helped Finley down, then dismounted. Martin appeared instantly to take the horses, and Ev paused only long enough to remove the saddlebags and pull Marty over for an embarrassed hug. Susan, his Susan, stood on the porch, waiting. He ran to her.

"I'm back," he whispered as he wrapped his weary, dust-coated arms around her.

Susan said nothing, but Ev knew what was in her heart by the tears which trickled down her cheeks and fell, warm and moist, onto his neck.

"It's good to be home," he said, choking with emotion.

"Home?" she asked, gazing around at the shambles of the station.

"Yes, home," he told her.

Later, when the horses were attended to, Martin returned and sat with Ev on the porch. By that time Ev had carried Todd and Rachel around the house twice.

"Go help your ma with dinner," Ev told the little ones.

Rachel dashed inside, and Todd followed somewhat reluctantly.

"You caught up with them, huh?" Marty said, touching the saddlebags.

"Yes, son," Ev said.

"Rip, too?"

"We buried 'em at Shaw's Crossin'."

"I figured you would, Pa, but I sort of hoped maybe Rip would get away."

"He was as guilty as the others, son."

"I know," Martin said, nodding his head sadly. "Still, I don't think his heart was really in it. He could've shot me. If he'd wanted, he could've tracked down Fin and the little ones. I like to think he didn't have any choice."

Ev started to argue, but something stopped him.

"You could be right," Ev answered instead. "He said before he died that he hoped you didn't bear him a grudge."

"I don't."

"What do you say we wash up for supper, son?"

"Sure, Pa," Marty said, leaning against Ev's side for a moment before scampering inside.

Susan remained silent through dinner. She did give thanks that Ev had returned safely, and she reminded the children to play quietly since their father had spent a long and difficult day and a half in the wild. But it wasn't until later, when the children were settled into their beds, that she led Ev outside. Together they stared overhead at a sky alive with stars.

"We've got an awful lot of work to do putting the house back into shape," Susan whispered. "Sarah Merritt sent over some tin plates, and Martin started carving me some wooden bowls and forks."

"There are some cups to replace, too."

"Yes."

"Mitch Burnett's sendin' a wire to Austin about Nolan. We'll be gettin' some reward money, maybe a thousand dollars all totaled. Maybe some more from the company. I recovered that payroll."

"Ev, I was so afraid we'd lose you this time. I was up half the night with the children, wiping tears and chasing away nightmares. Promise me you won't ever go away from us again."

"I can't, Susan," he said, trembling as he drew her face closer.

"Why?"

"Because there's always the chance I might have to leave in order to protect you. Because as long as there are any George Nolans in this world, one may happen along again."

"No, not ever again."

"We'll pray not. Susan, it was never my intention to come out here in order to hide from life. There are no guarantees that we can find a place that's ever completely safe."

"That's what frightens me," she whispered, sinking her face into his chest.

"Me, too. I worry one of the children could ride up to a neighbor's house and get shot like Tim Merritt. I worry about rattlesnakes and cholera, drought and flood. But I know we're strong enough to face whatever comes."

"Are we?" she asked. "You didn't hear Rachel screaming, didn't have to set her on your knee and tell her she's safe, tell her not Nolan or anyone else would harm her father."

"It may be my turn tonight," he said somberly. "It's been rough on all of us. We've bled, not on the outside where you can patch it with a bit of cloth and a dab of iodine, but inside, where the scars don't heal right away. All wounds mend, though. It'll take time. But somethin' good's come of this, too."

"Something good?" she asked, shaking with sudden rage. "Tell me what?"

"This," he said, turning toward the house. "This place. The sky overhead. Todd feedin' the chickens. Rachel tyin' a ribbon in her hair. Finley mendin' a harness, and Marty learnin' to shave. I know we'll never stand out here and stare at that swirl of dust creepin' up Calvary Hill without wonderin' if it isn't bringin' us some new peril. But we'll never take the new day for granted, either. I'll never hold you close without treasurin' the moment. I'll never look past my children without thankin' God that I'm here to be with them."

"Yes," Susan agreed, gazing overhead again. "You're right. I guess I have been guilty of overlooking the good things sometimes."

"We all do, Susan," Ev said, leading her back toward the house. "Until we experience something like what's just happened. I pray I'll never have the chance to learn this lesson a second time."

"Me, too," Susan whispered.

If you have enjoyed this book and would like to receive details of other Walker Western titles, please write to:

Western Editor
Walker and Company
720 Fifth Avenue
New York, NY 10019

FEB 87